THE MATRIARCH

By Kevin A. Ranson

This novel is a work of fiction. All of the events, characters, names and places depicted herein are fictional or used in fictitiously. No representation is made that any of the statements made in this novel are true or that any incident depicted in this novel actually occurred is intended or should be inferred by the reader.

THE MATRIARCH

ISBN 13: 978-0615803449
ISBN 10: 061580344X

Printed in the United States of America

Special thanks to Tara Mitchell, Dennis Wemm and
Kia Motors

Thanks also to my copyeditor, Brett J. Link,
and my proofreader, Linda S. Cowden

Chapter 1

It was unusually cold for the first Sunday of November. The sky was clear and the moon was full.

Just after midnight, an old man placed two rusty gas cans next to a plastic fuel container, all of them full, into the bed of his 1965 Ford pickup. The truck's red paint was scratched and faded. He kept the vehicle patched together with duct tape and coat hangers, but it still ran all right.

After locking up his trailer, he drove to the top of the hill and parked his truck just off the two-lane highway. Across the road was a one-room church next to a cemetery. No one used the church anymore, but headstones kept popping up next to it as the tiny West Virginia community continued to die.

With his good hand, he was able to carry the two cans together and still manage the plastic container in his weak one. He carried them to the other side of the road and looked up at the door to the old church.

It terrified him.

There was something inside, he'd been told. Something he wasn't supposed to look at and was sure he didn't want to see, but there was no one else around that could do what he needed to.

He didn't know who kept the key, so a carpenter's pry bar would serve instead. A piece of the crumbling doorframe broke free of the latch holding the padlock, allowing the door to swing open. He left the plastic fuel container outside and carried the cans in with him. It was so dark inside the room that he could barely make out where the pews were, and that suited him just fine.

Keeping his head down so he could only see his feet, he shuffled toward the front of the church and set one of the cans down to open the other. He poured it out onto the floor in a wide half circle, cringing at the acrid gasoline vapors. It gurgled at first as it emptied, then poured smoothly at the end. After he dropped the first can and went back for the second, he made a mistake, seeing something he meant not to.

Closer to the center aisle than he would have liked, there were feet dangling off the front end of the pew, as if someone were sitting and patiently waiting for him to complete his work.

He knew not to look up. He didn't want to see who it was or in what state they were in.

Regaining his composure, he uncapped the second can and poured it out as he backed toward the door, swishing it back and forth to cover as much of the floor as he could. Most of it was gone as he reached the back of the church, so he dropped the can and left the rest to spill out on its own.

The old man pulled the door shut again as he exited, then retrieved the plastic fuel container. He uncapped it and reversed the spout so he could pour it better.

All around the outside of the church, the old man

splashed the contents up the walls until he had emptied it. He stowed the nozzle back into the container and set it down, then took a box of safety matches from his flannel shirt pocket.

On his first try, he lit the church aflame. It caught quickly, fast enough that the old man felt the need to hurry, gathering up his empty container and crossing the highway back to his truck. Safe inside his vehicle with the windows up and the doors locked, the old man picked up the Bible he had brought with him from off the passenger seat. He held it close to his chest as he watched the church burn.

A police cruiser arrived minutes later. A young officer in plain clothes got out, saw the church, then saw the old man in the truck.

"Ed?" he called out. "Ed, did you see what happened?"

The old man didn't move, didn't unlock the door and didn't answer.

Another police car arrived. The first policeman went up to the older officer to report the situation.

"Arnie, Ed was here before I got here. He won't say anything. I can't even get him to open the door. He's holding his Bible and, I dunno, praying."

"Guess it was too much to expect the volunteer fire department to come out here after a Saturday night." He looked back at the younger officer with a confused expression. "Did you say Ed had a Bible?"

"Yeah. Why?"

"Ed's a 'Two-Sunday' man, Jim."

Jim didn't seem to get the reference.

"Only goes on Christmas and Easter." Arnie walked up to the red Ford and tapped on the window. "Open the door, Ed. We gotta talk."

Ed shook his head, looking frightened at even the suggestion.

There was a loud bang, then another that came from the church. Jim pulled his revolver.

Arnie waved him down. "Those are probably gas cans. The vapor trapped inside can cause them to pop off like that." He could see the plastic fuel container in the bed of Ed's truck. "I think Ed might know more about that. Ed, are you afraid of something out here?"

The old man nodded, shaking.

"Leave the door locked and crack the window so we can talk."

It seemed to be a good compromise for Ed. He cranked the window an inch down, then took hold of his Bible with both hands again.

Arnie gave Ed a stern look. "Tell me who set the church on fire."

Ed nodded. "I did, Arnie."

"Okay, then. Why?"

"He said he wouldn't leave if I didn't. I had to burn it to the ground."

"Who told you that?"

"He said he was the Devil."

It was laughable, but Ed wasn't laughing any more than Arnie was. Something had spooked a cranky old man into an act of arson, and Arnie was beginning to worry what it *really* was.

"And how did you know he was the Devil?"

"He was beautiful, Arnie, just like it says," he indicated the Bible, "but mostly, I just believed him when he said it."

Part of the roof caved in as the flames roared, but for an instant, Jim thought he saw something else in the flames. He looked back at Arnie who had seen the same thing.

"Ed? Was anyone inside the church when you set the fire?"

The old man looked down in shame and anguish, then raised his head and looked mournfully at the burning church.

"This little light of mine," Ed started to sing, "I'm gonna let it shine. Oh, this little light of mine, I'm gonna let it shine…"

Chapter 2

"...Let it shine, all the time, let it shine!"

The a capella church hymn sounded joyful even through the speaker of a mobile phone. For a woman in her nineties, Ruth had a beautiful voice.

Janiss busily packed a box with a few of her favorite mystery novels and a couple of textbooks she could look through if she really got bored. It was Saturday morning, and most of Goodwin Hall had already fled Glenville State College for a week-long Thanksgiving break.

The phone on her bed went silent. "Ruth?" Janiss asked clearly, listening to hear if her friend was still there.

"I'm here, dear. Did you enjoy my singing?"

"I always love your singing. Did they tell you I'm coming out to see you tomorrow?"

"Yes, they did!" the elderly woman answered with excitement. "Marley told me, but I have to see a specialist after breakfast. Would it be okay if you came to see me in the afternoon?"

"Of course," Janiss replied. "They're going to make you miss your church service?" Ruth loved her Sunday worship.

"The Lord will forgive me one Sunday, I suppose."

"I'd think so. Okay, see you then!"

"Be safe, dear. Bye!" The line clicked off.

There was a knock at the door to her dorm room, already propped open to let in some air. Janiss set her book box down on the bed and turned to look. A mocha-skinned young woman leaned in the doorway with her arms folded and looking catty. Her gold winter coat looked too warm for the weather, let alone for being inside.

"Hello, Felicia," Janiss greeted her before going back to her packing.

"Spoiled little rich girl still slumming out at that nursing home?" Felicia chided. "She must be a richer relative than your daddy *and* on her death bed."

Janiss looked harshly at Felicia. "Why?"

Felicia couldn't keep a straight face. "Oh, come on, Janiss! Stick up for yourself!"

Janiss sighed. "At least I'm not a stuck-up cheerleader sleeping with half the football team," she said without any enthusiasm.

Felicia looked genuinely hurt. "That was mean."

"I'm sorry," Janiss started to say, but then Felicia grinned.

"I'm still playing with you, but that was good! For the record, though, the other half of the football team is *not* worth sleeping with."

Janiss glanced at Felicia's coat again. "Already too cold for you?"

"Everything north of Miami is too cold," Felicia corrected. She took a moment to size up Janiss. "I guess I'd feel right at home, too, if I was an ice princess from Ohio. You know, with long raven hair, eyes like coal and skin as white as snow."

"My eyes and hair are brown, and I'm not that pale." Janiss resisted looking down at her hands, knowing Felicia was watching for it.

Felicia grinned, looking at the desk lamp. "I guess it must be the light in here." She flipped the overhead light on with the switch by the door. "Oh, yeah, you're right. They're just... brown." She made it sound disappointing.

Janiss tried ignoring her again, but being accused of having both pallid skin and bland hair made her feel self-conscious. She tried to sneak a look in a mirror, but Felicia caught her.

"If you look, I'll know it bothers you."

"I'm kind of busy, Felicia."

"You're always kind of busy."

"That's why I'm a straight-A student and you aren't."

Felicia beamed. "Better! But you already told me you got a B last semester, so you are officially no longer perfect."

Janiss pulled out a suitcase, unzipped it and started taking smaller matched bags out of it.

"I was wondering why you hadn't left yet." Then Felicia's eyes widened. "Did your daddy say yes?" She could hardly contain herself.

Janiss tried to look humble about it, but she couldn't keep from smiling.

"And he has no idea Danny is going out there with you?"

"Actually," Janiss admitted, "he insisted." It

bothered her a little, but at least her father had agreed.

"Oh. So your parents are like that, are they? You sure you're an only child?"

"He and mom are afraid something might happen if I'm out there alone."

"But he's not afraid of what will happen when you and Danny are out there by yourselves? With nothing to do in that old country house to stay warm?"

Janiss smiled a little but was amused enough to let Felicia go on wondering about it.

"You know, you have to be the big cat in the relationship, right?" Felicia brought her arms up and brandished her finger-curled hands like paws. She pretended to lick her hand and groom her hair with the back of it, then tiptoed around the room like she was stalking prey.

Janiss giggled. "You need to stop watching those animal shows."

"Not until I've seen them all," Felicia said and began narrating her pantomime. "The tigress chooses her mate, stalks him, then leads him back to her den of naughty things." She started to open one of the smaller suitcases Janiss had left closed. "Is this the one with the naughty things?"

Janiss batted Felicia's hand away.

Felicia hissed at her; it was pretty good.

"Danny and I are not officially a couple, just good friends." Janiss took the smaller case away and set it out of Felicia's reach.

"Uh huh. 'With benefits.'"

Janiss shrugged and grinned guiltily.

"I call 'bullshit!' He's the only guy you're ever with at any time, and heaven forbid anyone catches you outside of this room. Everyone already thinks you're a couple, so stop pretending."

"Why does anyone else care? It's none of their business."

"You've been away at college for three years. You know damn well everything going on here is everybody's business."

The next time Janiss looked over at Felicia, she was staring down at Janiss's feet.

"The boots, right?" Janiss asked. "Aren't they great?"

"Oh, they're nice. For stripper boots."

Janiss refused to take the bait and continued to pack.

After she finished, Felicia helped Janiss take the luggage out to Janiss's car. It was a brand-new "molten red" Kia Soul her father had bought her as an early graduation present: low profile tires, satellite radio, the works. It was a cute little vehicle, and Felicia was openly jealous of it.

"You don't deserve this," Felicia told her, acting like she was trying to hug it. "You should throw it away and leave me the keys. And this parking spot, too, because you'll never get it again once classes start back up."

Another car pulled up behind them and stopped in the street. It was a white, late 1990s Saturn coupe that was very low to the ground. Two young men sat inside.

"Your 'knight in white Saturn' has arrived," Felicia teased.

Janiss did a poor imitation of Felicia's hiss at her, mostly because the song she referenced was older than both of them put together. Janiss sashayed over to the passenger's side for Felicia's benefit – making fun of her, really – then leaned provocatively in the window as it powered open.

"Where are you boys off to?" she asked.

There was Daniel, wearing sunglasses on a cloudy day.

He was driving; it was his car, after all. His sandy hair needed a trim, but it wasn't too long yet and still cute. He was wearing his older brother's Navy pea coat and leather gloves, pretending he was trying to look cool for her. His friend, Randy, was riding shotgun and looking typically disheveled.

"Hey, gorgeous," Randy said to her. "Cute boots."

"You never come over to my window any more," Daniel said with one hand on the wheel. He looked down over his sunglasses at her with those ridiculously bright blue eyes of his.

Janiss arched an eyebrow at him. "Because it doesn't roll down."

"She's gotcha there!" Randy razzed him. "You need to get your shit fixed."

All the way from the sidewalk, Felicia yelled, "Kiss him!"

"Yeah, Janiss," Randy said with a smile. "Kiss me."

"Not you," Janiss retorted without trying to sound mean.

Janiss never thought of herself as a proverbial good girl, but she worried that she had been stringing Daniel along. He had been very patient and she appreciated that. Exploring those possibilities was the point of spending the week of Thanksgiving together at her family's old farm outside of town.

Giving Randy a devilish look, Janiss pushed herself through the window and leaned over to Daniel, meeting him halfway for an impromptu kiss.

"That tight little sweater," she heard Randy say, "right in my face. You're cruel, Janiss."

She slinked back out of the car window, blushing a bit while keeping eye contact with Daniel. Felicia was cheering behind her. Janiss turned and looked; people were starting to stare.

"You'll be back tonight?" Janiss asked Daniel.

"Just to Ripley and back. Should be out at the farm by sunset or sooner."

Randy shrugged. "Unless we kidnap him. Man-camp should be up and running by now. Ribs, chicken, beer and people running around in the woods with guns who never shoot anything. No man alive can resist."

Janiss grinned. "Well, call me if you're abducted."

Both Daniel and Janiss gazed across at one another, not saying a word for a short eternity.

Randy rolled his eyes. "Oh, for fuck's sake! Will *someone* just say 'I love you' so I can go home?"

They said nothing and just smiled at one another.

"You two are pathetic," Randy groaned. He put on a cheap pair of black sunglasses and pointed down the hill. "Hit it."

Janiss stepped away from the car just before they drove off. Felicia came up behind her, pretending to clap her hands.

"What's that for?" Janiss asked.

"A pathetic public display of affection, but a step in the right direction. Does Danny cuddle?"

Chapter 3

The sky was overcast and gloomy, but it didn't bother Janiss.

Central West Virginia was beautiful that time of year and it didn't hurt driving a new car over and through the mountains. She loved the sound the flat, wide tires made as they hummed across the single-lane asphalt road. Visible through the empty trees, fallen leaves spilled over from the forest floor onto the road and scattered in the wake of the vehicle's passing.

At the crest of a hill and around another turn her destination came into sight: a farm nestled in a small valley where three mountaintops came together.

The main road cut the property in half, with the farmhouse built into one of the hills. Narrow pine trees, originally planted along a fence that had been removed years before, ringed the front of the property. On the opposite side was a barn-sized utility building and a fenced-in garden with a wide creek running behind them.

Janiss slowed to a crawl and drove off onto a gas company road that followed a narrow creek up the hill. The gravel path doubled as a driveway back to the old garage behind the farmhouse. After she parked in the turnaround and shut off the engine, an eerie silence remained that was interrupted only by the sound of an occasional falling limb onto a bed of leaves.

The old farmhouse was at least a hundred years old, kept up and added to with whatever was around whenever repairs or additions were required. Shingles had been used for siding, while an aging tin roof kept the rain off. The back porch off of the kitchen was covered and partially walled in with latticework, with all manner of eclectic things hanging off of it. One side of the house was burrowed into the hillside, serving as a foundation for a furnished room upstairs and the walls of a kitchen cellar below.

Leaving everything in her vehicle, Janiss walked around from the backyard to the front, where the main entrance was. She unlocked the door to the screened-in porch with a simple key. An old antique key was required to open the main entry, a dark cherry door with a glass top half. It opened under its own weight with a loud creak, allowing the gloomy day to illuminate the dark interior. Janiss felt along the inside of the open door for the light switch and flipped it up.

It felt like home. It was Gramma's house.

Real wood molding framed the yellowed walls and doorways in and out of the living room. The furniture was old, but in good repair, from the couch and rocking chairs to the recliner positioned in front of a tiny Zenith television on a stand. A massive, metal gas heater was "the monster" that guarded the living room, alive with ceramic tiles inside that glowed whenever the heater came on.

The walls were sparsely decorated. One of Janiss's favorite pictures hanging there depicted a wintery night scene, sketched in chalk, of a cabin under the moon. Every time she saw it, it always managed to look crooked to her. Try as she might, she couldn't resist straightening it yet again.

Janiss shuffled out of her coat and draped it over the back of the recliner. Just inside the hallway into the kitchen was the corded house telephone – a necessity in the mountains, since mobile phones rarely worked that far back in the hills. Family pictures hung on the wall across from the telephone, placed there so Gramma could see who she was talking to.

Her mom told her that the phone used to be a "party line" with multiple homes sharing one number. The service remained spotty, especially in the wintertime, even after each house was assigned a dedicated number. Janiss checked for a dial tone and was happy to hear one.

Flipping on the light, Janiss found the kitchen as it always was: cluttered yet organized. Most the appliances were new, including the gas cooking stove, refrigerator and microwave. The high-tech items clashed the paper-yellow walls and white-painted coarse-wood molding. The windows looking into the backyard were framed with tacky flower-print curtains. Looking through the latticework enclosing most of the back porch, she smiled at how good her little car looked in front of the old garage.

Besides the back door, there were three other doors out of the kitchen: one led to the ugly pink bathroom; another the enclosed side porch, where the freezer and dryer were kept; and the last to the in-ground cellar.

Janiss loved the cellar. She didn't know why.

A few of Gramma's inspirational counter cross stitches hung on the outer door to the cellar. Among her favorites was one with a number of sayings: "If it spills, clean it," "If it starves, feed it" and the one she loved the most, "If it cries, love it."

Turning the knob to the cellar, she pulled the white door open to reveal an unpainted second door behind it – a clever way to create an old-world boundary to keep the inside cooler. She gave the second door a firm push, opening it into a rough bricked room. A tiny opaque window in a high corner was the only part of the cellar interior that didn't have solid earth behind the wall. She stared into the darkness and let the cool air waft over her, the smell of stone, earth and the contents of old canning jars taking her back in time.

For a moment, Janiss was a little girl again and her grandparents were still alive. Gramma was the best cook. She would remake last night's mashed potatoes into fried potato cakes served with fresh eggs from the chicken coop. Sometimes there would also be a side of "Grampa sausage" her Grampa made himself. She found out later how the sausage was made and lost her taste for it; but it was all a happy part of spending her summers and holidays in the mountains.

Switching the light on from outside the cellar, the memories disappeared when her gaze fell on the mostly empty shelves in the room. A folding table in the center held bottled water, an empty Styrofoam cooler and sugared sodas left over from when her parents were there the previous summer.

After clicking off the light and closing the cellar doors, Janiss unlatched the back door and pulled it open. Behind the screen door stood a man with piercing eyes and a dirt-streaked face staring creepily into the kitchen.

Janiss gasped, then realized who he was.

She had only ever heard his name given as Caleb, the son of a family that used to live a few farms down the road, which, in West Virginia terms, equaled more than a few miles. He had the wide-eyed, unblinking stare of a child hidden behind an unwashed face. His baseball cap and layers of clothes looked like he slept in them, the colors muted into shades of brown and gray. He smelled like the road, a combination of sweat, weather and whatever he had trudged through walking from house to house.

"Caleb!" Janiss scolded, using the tone her Gramma had taught her. "You know better than to stand there like that!"

Caleb blinked once, nodded and stepped back.

Her parents had always been afraid that Caleb could be dangerous. While he was only a little taller than Janiss, he was easily twice her weight and had huge, muscular hands – the kind that looked like they could strangle people two at a time if he could only catch them. Janiss couldn't explain why, but she felt Caleb was an innocent who would never consciously hurt anyone. At the same time, he was a drifter – and the family who once lived down the road had moved away leaving him for the rest of the farms to care for.

"Are you hungry?" Janiss asked in a more caring tone.

For a moment, he dared to look into her eyes. When he looked away, he nodded again as if he was ashamed to have done so.

"Step away from the door and back into the yard so I can get to my car."

Caleb obeyed, shuffling into the middle of the backyard. Janiss unlatched the screen door and walked out to her car, keeping an eye on Caleb while walking confidently. She took a box of groceries from the back of the vehicle, all items that needed refrigeration, then closed the hatchback and carried them in.

As she had seen her Gramma do, Janiss turned the well water knob to "on" and unfurled a few yards of the garden hose connected at the back porch. Already seeming to know what was expected of him, Caleb held out his hands while Janiss sprayed them clean. Well, at least, cleaner. After a few moments, Janiss turned off the water, gathered a few of the apples she had bought at the store and pressed them into Caleb's hands.

Caleb greedily bit into one of them, then dared another look at Janiss. She smiled at him, but he didn't smile back. She wondered if he even could.

"Okay, now – go on! No more lurking in doorways."

Nodding, Caleb pocketed the other apples and continued on his way. Janiss went inside, latched the kitchen doors again and went to the front windows.

From the porch, she watched as Caleb lumbered down the road from whence she had just come, eating his apples.

She neither hated him nor disliked him, but he seriously creeped her out.

As soon as she was sure he was around the bend up the road, Janiss made more trips to her car for the rest of the groceries and her luggage. After tying her hair back with a colorful scrunchie, she looked over the cleaning supplies in the cupboard of the ugly pink bathroom.

"Time for a little homemaking," she said with a grin.

Chapter 4

Plopping down into the recliner across from the tiny television in the living room, Janiss adjusted the wall-mounted lamp behind her. She had spent almost three hours cleaning, mostly in the kitchen and bathroom, but she also gave the rest of the farmhouse a quick dusting and vacuuming.

From where she sat in the living room, she could see through the porch windows, across the front yard and over the road past the mailbox. The at-dusk security light over the utility building was just kicking on. It felt different being there alone in the fall, with no one around and no insects chirping, but it didn't frighten her.

The sun was down, but where was Daniel?

She knew Randy would tempt him into staying the night. It was the reason she had given him the out since they had the rest of the week and the following weekend ahead of them. Daniel would either show up or call, so she wasn't too worried.

It was going to be cool that night, so Janiss had cranked up the monster heater a few notches in the living room. The periodic whooshing sound it made whenever the thermostat kicked it on was always comforting to her. She picked up a favorite book, turned it the first page, and began to read.

So, of course, the house telephone rang.

Janiss sighed, smiled, put her book down and got up to answer the phone. It was weird not to reach into her pocket for her phone, but the clear ringing bell of an actual wall-mounted telephone was all a part of the charm of staying at Gramma's house. Sadly, her mobile phone was useless for holding a signal this deep in the mountains.

"Hello?" Janiss was fairly certain who it was.

"Greetings from man-camp!" a cheery voice shouted. In the background, she could hear hooping and hollering, the collective roar of inebriated hunters getting ready for the start of hunting season thirty-six hours too early.

"Are on your cell?"

"Yep!"

"You're supposed to be here."

"What?"

In the background, she heard someone call out, "Is that your girlfriend, Danny Boy?"

While he had a mute button he could have used, Janiss could hear the attempted muffling of the phone against some article of clothing. Hasty explanations were being exchanged along with spotty excuses, so Janiss patiently waited – although she wasn't entirely sure why.

Finally, the call resumed. "Janiss? You still there?"

"Funny. I was going to ask you that, *Daniel.*"

Janiss had known Daniel Allan Moore since grade school. He had always been a decent guy and she knew far more about him than she probably had any right to. When they wound up at the same college in West

Virginia, they had been an on-again/off-again couple. Daniel wanted to get serious and Janiss wanted to graduate, so she kept him at arms length and he seemed content to wait. There were nights when things got very close that ended with them going to breakfast together, but Janiss often pulled away after nights like that. Whether they were together or apart, they had always remained good friends and Janiss trusted him.

The deal she made with her father, unfortunately, was that Daniel was supposed to be there, and he hadn't even left yet. She wasn't that surprised.

"I got caught up," Daniel explained. "Randy and his folks invited me up for a round."

She heard Randy in the background. "And my uncles, and my cousins and all their kids..."

"You're drinking?" Janiss accused.

Daniel stammered. "I'm legal."

"Dad said I could use Gramma's place this week but not alone. You being here at night was kind of a condition."

"Do you want me to drive there from Ripley tonight? I can get there in two hours."

"After a few beers? Through Spencer at night on Route 33? Don't you dare!"

"Ah," Daniel mused, "that's concern I hear."

"You should be so lucky," Janiss dismissed. "If Dad asks, you were here. Sleep it off, come out tomorrow afternoon. You can meet me at the nursing home."

Daniel started feigning coughs. "Old people live there! Who knows what diseases they have. People die in those places, you know."

"Your punishment should fit the crime, right? I'm going to see Ruth around three. If you don't want to come out, meet me here around dinner."

"Are you cooking? I'll take my chances not dying at the old folks home."

Janiss was getting irritated at the bravado in front of the other guys listening in, so she decided to up the ante. "Nope. You're cooking. Steaks. You know what I like."

"Fillet of minion? Where am I going to find a minion by tomorrow?"

Janiss grinned. "You know where the key is. Medium. Don't burn my dinner or you'll be sleeping in the outhouse. It smells wonderful this time of year."

After a pause, Daniel conceded. "Yes, ma'am," he replied, accompanied by the roar of laughter and inappropriate comments. "See you tomorrow!"

"Have fun, sleep well, drive safe."

Janiss hung up the phone, paused a moment, then sat down again with her book. She smiled at the thought of Daniel falling all over himself to try and cook for her, knowing full well that he would, and she intended to reward him for his effort.

Chapter 5

"How fast can you get here, Craig?"

It had been foolish to just take off in the middle of the night, but the last line of the novel-length text he'd received from Amy was justification enough. He hadn't known she had been recently divorced or even that she still knew his number, but the invitation had been clear.

Barreling down the highway, Craig was all smiles. Between the small towns and the occasional residential utility light, only the powerful glow of high-tech headlights illuminated the empty road twisting ahead of him.

Amy's out-of-the-blue text had arrived while he was at the dealership the previous evening finalizing the paperwork on his first new vehicle: a fully loaded black Cadillac Escalade. Everything inside the vehicle was pristine and it was all *his*. The combination of a fresh opportunity with his old flame and desperately wanting to play with his new toy was irresistible.

His plan was simple. Showing up on a Sunday morning for brunch wouldn't have had the impact of actually appearing in the flesh hours after her text. He didn't even bother to answer her; showing up at her doorstep would be his response. Why else give him her new address unless she was at least hoping he would?

Craig took another sip from his insulated mug. It

was almost half empty, about the point where the coffee was still hot but not scalding. All the cream and sugar that had settled into the bottom made each subsequent drink all the sweeter. If the coffee failed to keep him awake for the next hour, the cold night air would do the trick. He pushed a button on his door and lowered the driver's side window about an inch.

After accelerating out of a curve, Craig glanced down at his dashboard. The Escalade was just about to turn over its first hundred miles. He grinned as he repeatedly sneaked looks down at the dash trying to catch the number rolling over. Just as it did, he looked back at the road in time to see something on the right side of the vehicle fall into its path.

Impact.

Craig gripped his steering wheel and stomped on his brake; the Escalade skidded to a stop in an impressively short distance. After shifting into park, the shoulder strap on his seat belt disengaged. He wondered for a moment why the airbags never inflated before finally assuming that whatever he'd hit hadn't been big enough to set off them off.

What the hell was that?

He could make out something brownish and furry slumped over in the middle of the road ahead of him, just below the hood where he couldn't see it clearly. He considered backing up enough to look from inside, but he also wanted to know if there was any damage. The thought alone pissed him off: that his first brand-new vehicle was already fucked up because Bambi or someone's dog didn't have enough sense to stay out of the road.

Flipping his hazard lights on, Craig glanced into his rearview mirror and then up the road. No other cars were coming. He could take a quick look and, if it was nothing, just hose it off later. The thought of seeing splattered blood and guts all over the front end disgusted him.

He got out and walked around to the front, discovering that the dead thing in road was a fawn. It was barely bigger than a good-sized dog. He looked at the grill of the Escalade, but there was no visible damage or even that much blood.

Lucky, but weird.

Taking a step closer, Craig saw the fawn's coat had blood on it around the back of its neck and on its haunches. What disturbed him was that much of the animal's damage was around the throat, like something had ripped it out. Shouldn't it have been bleeding out more if he'd caused that by hitting it? The carcass was taking up enough of the right lane to mess up any other vehicle speeding around the corner. If he could find something to drag it off to the side of the road with, he might not actually have to touch it.

"You okay, buddy?" a disturbingly cheerful voice said from behind him. "You have that deer-in-the-headlights look."

Spooked, Craig wheeled around. Partially blinded from the Escalade's headlights, he could just make out the silhouette of a sizable man. Enough light spilled over from the high beams to reveal blood-stained hands. Each time the hazard lights blinked on, Craig saw a devilish grin getting wider.

What the hell was wrong with his eyes?

There was a blur of movement, a flash of pain and nothing more.

Chapter 6

Janiss signaled and turned onto Route 5 running between Sand Fork and Glenville. The skies were darker than a normal Sunday mid-afternoon, and the temperatures were still falling. The roads were mostly empty except for the occasional orange-capped hunters in their oversized trucks driving here and there. It took about fifteen minutes to reach the split-lane just outside of town, the one that turned over a bridge onto the most unfortunately named road in Gilmer County.

Butcher's Run was what the locals called the road long before the Feds topped a mountain flat and built a correctional facility there. Janiss laughed every time she passed the state road signs that read "Warning: Prison Road. Do not pick up hitchhikers." Was that really a problem?

What few people knew was that Butcher's Run continued on for another mile or so, ending at a facility with a different purpose. Cedarcrest Sanctum was a modern nursing home, but famously private. It was run by a secretive administrator who was rumored to accept or turn away new residents on a whim. Those who made it inside raved about the care they received. The rumor, of course, was that anyone who passed away in their care was hushed up, as if it was something terrible to receive great care just before you died of natural causes.

At the end of the road was a turnaround big enough for a tractor trailer, with an unoccupied gatehouse and call box just on the left. The gate was wide enough for two large vehicles to pass side by side. A pair of gray brick columns topped with security camera domes supported the automatic black iron gates. Janiss lowered her car window and leaned out to press the call button on the speaker box and waited for the red light to illuminate.

"Welcome to Cedarcrest. State your name and business, please." The feminine voice was stern but not unpleasant.

"Janiss Connelly. I'm here to see Ruth White."

"Hello again, Ms. Connelly. Ruth asked about you this morning. Park anywhere on the right visitor's landing, please."

The callbox light went out and the gates silently swung open. Janiss maneuvered her Kia over the drainage grating that ran beneath the gates when they were in the closed position, listening for the familiar clacking sound as each tire rolled over it. There was a gradual curve up to the hilltop and guest parking area.

Looking like a fortress of sandstone bricks and mirrored glass, it wasn't difficult to tell that Cedarcrest Sanctum wasn't entirely a nursing home. The three-story square central tower was the cornerstone of the facility, looming over a split entryway of glass doors. The building extended off in opposite directions from the tower, with a single-story wing off to the left and a two-story wing to the right. The landscaping was immaculate, resembling the grounds of a hotel inside of a theme park.

Sadly, even on a Sunday, there were almost never any other visitors. There were designated parking spots in the front for two-dozen vehicles, but hers was often the only one parked there week after week. She assumed the staff must be parked around the sides in a private lot; but with no one else in sight, everything seemed very lonely from the outside.

After parking, she took her purse and a colorful gift bag out of her car before hurrying up the right ramp to the second set of sliding glass doors into the tower lobby. Set into the cement landing in front of the doors was an intricate circular design: a series of faces that resembled Mayan or Aztec masks. It took up the entire landing and was so huge that there was no physical way to cross the landing without stepping on some part of the circular seal design.

Janiss thought the little masks were grotesque when she first saw them, but she had grown fond of the little goggle-eyed fang faces since then. The design was also heavily used in the lobby overlooking the waiting area, tiled on three walls inside as if guarding the interior.

The theme park hotel motif continued inside as well, with carpeting everywhere and recessed lighting fixtures. Hallways extended out from both sides of the lobby. The main desk was staffed with the usual four-to-six people in monochromatic scrubs. Three sets of elevator doors were behind the main desk.

"Ms. Connelly?" the middle-aged woman behind the desk asked. It was the same voice as over the call box. Janiss recognized the nametag and smiled pleasantly.

"Hi, Yolanda! Is Ruth done with her appointment?"

Yolanda returned the smile, but there was a hint of something amiss. "I'm sorry, Ms. Connelly, but I didn't know until you just came in..."

Janiss looked horrified. "Is she okay?"

"What? No!" Yolanda shook her head. "I mean yes, she's fine. I'm so sorry I didn't explain that better. She's been moved into the private wing following her tests this morning."

The so-called "private wing" was where everyone Janiss came to see kept disappearing into, starting about two years before – a place where they were abruptly moved where they weren't supposed to have any visitors.

On multiple occasions, Janiss had asked to speak with the administrator about it; but she was neither given that person's name nor an audience. She even considered calling someone about investigating Cedarcrest, but she didn't know what she would tell them other than that she was frustrated and suspicious.

"I don't suppose asking to see the administrator again would do any good, right?"

To Janiss's surprise, Yolanda didn't outright refuse her. "Let me see if someone is available." She started typing something into her computer terminal and looked as if she were waiting on a response.

Janiss waited patiently, hoping the answer would be yes but fully expecting a no.

"Okay," Yolanda said. "The administrator is actually in Ruth's room right now supervising the transfer of her belongings. You can go down the hall and right on in."

Yolanda seemed to have carefully worded that response. Janiss still had no name and wasn't sure if the mysterious Ruler of Cedarcrest was a man or a woman. Why all the secrecy?

"Thank you," Janiss replied, less enthusiastically. "I know the way, if that's all right."

"You're trusted here, Ms. Connelly. Let us know if you need anything."

"Thank you. You all do a wonderful job here."

The décor of the lobby continued into the more public, non-private wing. After passing a pair of elevators and small utility room doors, the long carpeted hallway was well suited for a stroll. Windows down the right side provided a perfect view of the beautiful walking gardens outside behind the facility. It seemed a crime that no one was out there enjoying the day in spite of the oncoming cold. In fact, she had never seen anyone out there except for the one time she and Ruth had toured it themselves.

As Janiss walked down the hall toward Ruth's room, she remembered two other people she used to see from time to time. The first was John, or "Mr. Fisher" as he demanded to be called. He always seemed angry, but his temper was rarely flared around Janiss, especially after she proved herself unaffected by his complaining. The other was Vivian Johnson, a sweet lady who had trouble breathing and spoke very little. Janiss had read to her when she visited and Vivian seemed to enjoy it very much. Both Mr. Fisher and Vivian had been moved to the private wing, so Janiss never saw them around anymore. As she walked along, she noticed that many of the rooms were empty.

The second-to-last room down the hall belonged to Ruth. Janiss could hear her singing to herself as she drew closer. Didn't they say she wasn't there?

As Janiss entered the room, it was indeed empty. The bed was made, the shelves were vacant, and the little toys that Ruth kept on the windowpane were gone. On the wooden dresser next to the bed was a cardboard box with a few small belongings and an old push-button tape recorder next to it, the kind that used cassettes. The singing was coming from there.

Looking around, Janiss saw no one about. She pressed the stop button, and everything went silent. Confused, Janiss backed out of Ruth's old room and briskly walked down the hall toward the front of the home, almost running into an orderly she recognized leaving another room.

"Marley, where's Ruth?" Janiss asked.

Marley was an older gentleman himself. Janiss often wondered why someone almost as old as the people at the home was working there, but Marley seemed as spry as any of the staffers.

"They moved her to the private wing. Didn't they tell you at the desk?"

Janiss looked at him suspiciously. "Why does everyone I meet in here disappear into the private wing? What's so special in there?"

At that exact moment, Ruth's singing started again.

Marley appeared every bit as puzzled about the music starting again as Janiss. Determined to catch whoever started playing the tape again, she turned and quickly walked back down the hall with Marley close behind.

Inside was a middle-aged woman, perhaps in her fifties, looking regal in a dark, tailored suit. Her long hair was golden, but with a silvery sheen. She was very beautiful for her age – yet it was her presence that was compelling, like a movie star of whom no one had ever heard. For a few moments, all Janiss could do was stare in wonder. The woman was ethereal and Janiss was at a loss to explain why.

"Ms. Connelly, I presume?" the woman asked.

Janiss's voice failed her. The woman's blue-gray eyes were piercing, the eyes of someone used to being respected and obeyed. Unable to speak, Janiss merely nodded.

"Good," the woman replied. "My name is Louisa Newcomb, the administrator here at Cedarcrest. Ruth was under my care and I understand you were her only visitor. Have I been misinformed?"

"No, ma'am," Janiss answered, surprising herself.

It felt like a cloud had formed in Janiss's mind. Where did "ma'am" come from? Janiss didn't even call her own mother "ma'am" unless she was in real trouble. What was going on? Looking back for Marley, Janiss found him absent. It was only the two of them and Ruth's voice on the tape.

Louisa pressed the stop button again. "Ruth made

this tape for you when we told her the circumstances of her admission," she said, indicating the tape recorder. "Did you want it?"

"Yes," Janiss eagerly answered. "She was my friend."

"Most people your age avoid retirement homes the way they do hospitals. It reminds them of their mortality. What are you, twenty?"

Janiss smiled. "Twenty two." She hadn't meant to smile, but Louisa's spell over her felt like it was breaking. She was already feeling accused and defensive, and any mistake Louisa made felt like a small victory.

Louisa continued her impromptu interrogation. "You've nothing better to do on a weekend than visit an old woman on her death bed?"

Important or not, the icy tone had pushed Janiss as far as she was going to allow. "She's a *person*," Janiss fired back. "Do you see this place as just some kind of a business? Is that why so many of these rooms are empty?"

The administrator narrowed her gaze at Janiss. In turn, Janiss fought the urge to look away and stood her ground. Sure, it might be the last time she was allowed at Cedarcrest, but she would make damn sure no one else lined the pockets of a witch like Louisa Newcomb while she was running it.

An instant later, Louisa's expression broke with a bright smile, as though the entire exchange had been a joke. "There. That's what I was looking for. There's the lion behind the mouse."

Taken aback, Janiss asked, "Excuse me?"

"Passion. Or compassion. Both – or whichever. You've lost people close to you, haven't you? Grandparents, perhaps?"

Janiss nodded, shook off a flood of memories, then went back on the offensive. "What goes on in the private wing?"

"Also very direct," Louisa mused. "I'm afraid that only residents and staffers have access to the private wing and its secrets. It is simply impossible for you to be a resident, so you leave me no choice but to hire you if you want to learn more."

Janiss started to say something else before she realized what Louisa had said. "Hire? Me?" It didn't make any sense.

"Full time. Starting tomorrow if you like, or perhaps after the holiday?"

"I'm still in school. At Glenville."

Louisa smiled. "I went there once, a long time ago. Teaching?"

"Yes," Janiss answered. "I want to finish."

"Part time," Louisa countered. "Whenever you can, as many hours as you like – and I pay a generous wage. If you could fill out a few papers, we can get started with a tour of the private wing immediately after you sign our non-disclosure. Would you accompany me to my office?"

Janiss sensed it was all wrong.

Whether it was the sudden generous offer, or the exchange of words prior to it, Louisa Newcomb was not what she appeared. If Ruth was in any kind of trouble,

Janiss thought, it couldn't hurt to hear the rest of the pitch and find out just how deep of a hole the administrator of Cedarcrest could dig herself into.

"Sure, I'd love to," Janiss replied.

Chapter 7

Daniel was making good time. His Saturn coupe hugged the back roads of West Virginia as the hills rose and fell. He loved Route 33, a two-lane highway between Ripley and Glenville. For most of the road, the speed limit was around fifty-five; but he always pushed it a bit faster to see how quickly he could get back to school.

It was late already and the sky was getting dark fast, too. He still had to get to the grocery store for steaks before they closed and Janiss was going to be mad enough at him for not starting back sooner.

Daniel and Randy had talked for a while after Janiss had hung up. He knew he should have never told Randy anything about their relationship to begin with, but he was still afraid to say anything to Janiss directly.

"I like her," he had told Randy. "A lot."

Randy, of course, gave him crap for it. "So you're in 'like' with her. Like a sister?"

"No, but I think she sees me like a brother."

"That's a problem, dude."

Randy wasn't wrong. Every time Janiss pushed him away Daniel couldn't stop thinking about her, falling into old routines until she noticed him again. It wasn't like she ever dated anyone else.

Randy had an answer for that, too. "You know how to get over the last girl, right? Get on the next one. You need to think outside of her box."

Daniel smiled at that comment before imagining what Janiss would have thought if she'd heard it.

With the town of Spencer fresh in his rearview mirror, Daniel stopped at a small gas station. There were trucks of all sizes and shapes parked there, many painted in camouflage for the opening of hunting season the next morning. Each appeared equipped with a four wheeler and a gun rack. Daniel figured those came standard with the "hillbilly hunting package" at the dealer.

After authorizing his debit card and filling up, Daniel went inside to use the bathroom and grab a Diet Coke. Hunters wearing bright orange caps were loading up their coolers from every aisle, some bragging about how many points this buck had or how many does they kept seeing but couldn't shoot since they weren't in season. For most states, Thanksgiving was just a day of eating and football followed by a weekend of early Christmas shopping; in West Virginia, it was also a week-long celebration of shooting things.

As Daniel waited in line to pay for his drink, one of the hunters looked him up and down, grinned at his buddy, then spoke.

"Long way from the shoreline, ain't ya?"

Daniel thought about it, then realized the hunter was talking about what he was wearing. "It's my brother's pea coat. He's in the Navy."

The hunter and his buddy nodded in approval. "Thank him for his service next time you see him."

"Thanks. I will." That was different, but not unexpected.

Daniel nodded, paid and went out to his car. The Saturn was white with a black roof, which kind of stuck out next to all of the hunting trucks. Daniel imagined everyone was watching him, the only one not preparing to be in the woods at dawn on Monday morning; he fully intended to be fast asleep until at least nine.

It took him two tries to start the car. The starter was going and Daniel hadn't had the time or money during school to get it fixed. It was by far not the only problem the car had: the driver's window didn't go down more than two inches, the air conditioning didn't work and the engine started overheating if the car sat in traffic too long. Fortunately, it was cold outside and the heater worked fine – plus the gas mileage, along with no car payment, made it more than worth keeping.

A few minutes later, Daniel was clear of the town and back up to speed. As he cruised up the road, he took the time to enjoy the scenery as he drove. Unlike Route 50 through Clarksburg down I-79, the most direct route to Glenville State College was through the middle of the state. His dad had driven down the same roads years before and had shown Daniel pictures of the old gas stations that had been closed or abandoned long ago. Before billboards and interstate roads, ads like "Mail Pouch Tobacco" were painted on the sides of barns. But most of the working farms, like the barns themselves, weren't there anymore.

The other things that marked the trip were the one-room churches and hillside graveyards all along the route. Every ten miles or so was another community with a disappearing population too small to call a town. Each one seemed to have a sign with the area's name, that it was incorporated and a certified business location. Except for the holidays, young people didn't stay; there just weren't the kinds of jobs around that kids went to college for. When their parents or grandparents passed away, their homes went up for sale but usually stood empty – and so the cemeteries grew a little larger.

It was kind of depressing.

Daniel shook it off, worked the cap off of his Diet Coke and took a swig. Glancing at his watch, it was almost four in the afternoon, so he decided to text Janiss how far along he was before he lost the cell signal again. Reception was spotty away from the interstate highways and you never knew if or when the signal would drop.

Fumbling to get at his phone, Daniel pushed back on his seat to better position himself to fish it out of his jeans pocket without having to pull over. With one hand, he managed to call up Janiss's number and initiate a text. After missing a letter three times on the touchscreen, he glanced back at the road just as he reached the top of a hill going into a hairpin turn – and he was about to miss it.

Dropping his phone, he tapped the foot brake and pulled his emergency brake, cutting the wheel back and forth over the loose gravel as he left the road. With only a few feet before the hillside, he cut the steering wheel to the side, thankfully slow enough not to flip the car. The Saturn slid sideways up to the rail, just inches from actually impacting it.

Prying his hands off the leather-wrapped steering wheel, he calmly turned off the key, retrieved his phone from the passenger seat floor where it had fallen and got out. Walking up to the railing, he looked over the mountainside into an abyss ending in a valley of trees. He noticed the guardrail had been repaired a few times at least; if he hadn't stopped, he wouldn't have been alone down there.

"Damn."

He had to have a picture of *that* and snapped the hillside with his phone's camera. Besides, it'd be fun to send it along with a message to Janiss.

While he was stopped, he noticed a cemetery up ahead next to a blackened building that must have recently burned down. He thought it might have been a church, but he wasn't sure.

Chapter 8

One mystery had been solved already: the third-floor rooms at the top of the tower over the lobby were Louisa's offices.

The central elevator behind the main desk was the way up, accessed by a special key card. A short hallway connected the elevator to the main office itself with several smaller rooms off to either side.

The administrator's office was decorated in shades of alternating black and silver. A gray-tinted glass desk occupied the center of the room, a clever construct with angled tubes to the floor that hid wires for lighting and devices, including two laptops. On either side of the room were workstations, complete with power ports and LED lighting. The windows behind the desk overlooked the front of Cedarcrest, from the circular seal in front of the main doors all the way to the gatehouse. Beyond that was a breathtaking view of the mountains.

It was hard for Janiss to finish the paperwork she had been given with so much to distract her, but it was the only way she'd be able to see Ruth again.

The clear clipboard contained a small stack of papers. The first was a non-disclosure agreement, forbidding her from legally talking to anyone about anything at Cedarcrest under penalty of law. The second was a standard employment application that Louisa assured her was merely a formality. The last two papers were a W-4 tax form and a watermarked paper with a detachable check for five thousand dollars with Janiss's name already on it.

She didn't like putting her information on the employment form any more than she wanted to sign the NDA, but the worst case scenario was that she would call her father and let him know what was going on. Except for Louisa, it was only her elderly friends disappearing into the private wing that seemed sinister; everyone else she had met at Cedarcrest was caring, polite and professional.

One of the side doors opened. Louisa entered, along with a thin man in a dark blue business suit, with short blond hair and a stern look. The man stood to the side of the door and closed it behind them as Louisa walked over to Janiss.

"This is Timothy, my assistant. I trust everything is in order?"

Janiss had spent almost as much time thinking about how she was going to fool Louisa as she had being distracted by the view. She decided it was best to play cute and dumb.

"Wow," Janiss said. "I'm sorry, it's all I can come up with."

Louisa smiled. "Hold onto that word. You may need it again today."

She reached for the clipboard. Janiss handed it over, Louisa glanced over it, then removed the check and gave it to Janiss.

"This part you keep."

"Sorry. I mean, thank you, but I don't want to accept that just yet. I still haven't made up my mind."

Louisa looked hard at Janiss, as if trying to read her mind. She then handed the clipboard with the check to her assistant before looking back to Janiss. "The NDA will do for now. Follow me."

Through another door next to the wall of workstations, Louisa walked just ahead of Janiss down a short stairwell into the second floor of the private wing. The hallway was partially illuminated by side lighting and augmented with heavily tinted skylights above; with rooms on both sides of the hallway, there were no other windows. As Janiss had guessed, the private wing was as posh as the rest, more like a five-star hotel or luxury condo than a nursing home. Each had a stately door with brass numbering.

Halfway down the corridor were two recreational rooms, one on either side. Unlike the solid condo doors, these rooms had glass door fronts. The one on the left had shades drawn, but the room on the right was full of elderly folks, including two she immediately recognized. Louisa stepped aside and held the door to allow Janiss to enter first.

"Mr. Fisher! Vivian!" Janiss could hardly believe it. They looked great, and Mr. Fisher was out of bed. How was he standing up on his own when he couldn't walk before?

"Just call me John, my dear," Mr. Fisher replied. "It's good to see you again."

Janiss gave both of her old acquaintances quick

hugs, then noticed how everyone was looking at her. It was as if she was the most important person in the room, or possibly the one that something terrible was about to happen to. It all seemed too well and good, as though something sinister lurked beneath the surface of the situation.

Then it dawned on her: it was their movement. None of them were doddering or shuffling about. Their actions were quick and deliberate, like a younger person's movement. Janiss imagined that people half their age might have been wearing the masks of the people they had become. What was happening? Janiss looked back toward Louisa, who was conferring again with her thin assistant.

"Questions?" Louisa asked, looking toward her potential new employee.

"What's happened to everyone?"

The group chuckled together, a few even patting Janiss on the back or arm in reassurance, exactly the way an older person does when they believe someone doesn't understand something that they clearly do. Afterward, they looked to Louisa silently for her to answer the question for Janiss.

"It's a specialized treatment, one we're pioneering here at Cedarcrest. Not everyone is a candidate, but everyone you see here has responded positively to it. Ruth is our most recent patient to be accepted into the program. This is all still experimental, hence the need for secrecy."

Janiss nodded cautiously, but dared to be a bit

optimistic. "Is this some kind of stem cell research?"

Louisa shook her head slightly. "It's organic, but not stem cell related. The source is very precious, almost unique, something akin to a supplement. It has restorative properties, cognitive and physical. Years of research will be required to determine the long-term effects, but it looks promising."

"Is it anti-aging? Does it extend their lives?"

"All in due time, Janiss. Perhaps you would prefer to know exactly what I hired you for?"

Louisa looked over at Vivian.

"I want to follow my grandchildren online. What social networks should I use?"

Janiss smiled pleasantly. "Wouldn't you rather just talk to them?"

Vivian shrugged. "They don't talk anymore. They just peck away at their phones when I see them at all."

There were periodic bursts of laughter, some even boisterous, as side conversations spontaneously erupted about kids these days, how no one called, and other things that weren't like they used to be. The remarks overall, however, were positive; these people wanted to learn new things. There was passion in the room, an exuberance that could only be called youthful.

It was wonderful, but it wasn't right.

Louisa motioned for Janiss to follow her out. "I believe Janiss will be back later this week or next," she announced to the room, "so you can save up your questions for then."

The group waved and said goodbyes as Janiss

exited the room with Louisa. After the door shut, Louisa nodded to her assistant again, who left the two of them alone in the hall to walk back up to Louisa's office.

"Wow," Janiss said again.

"Impressed?"

"Concerned. When are they allowed to die?"

Louisa abruptly stepped in front of Janiss, blocking her path. "Who are you to make that determination?"

Janiss looked carefully into Louisa's eyes. "Aren't *you*? What if this wonder drug wears off? What if you cut them off? And if it works forever, are they immortal? No one has to die again, ever?" Janiss realized she was being a little over-dramatic with her comment, but what else was the point?

Unfazed by the absurdity of the suggestion, Louisa smirked. "Would that be so terrible?"

"I'm sorry, but it doesn't seem right."

"Very well. Let's discuss that further in my office."

After climbing back up into the office, Louisa offered Janiss a seat and checked something on one of her laptops.

"I understand," she continued as she looked over the screen. "You're young, Janiss. You don't understand what growing old is like. Your mind keeps telling you that you can do everything you used to do, but your body betrays you. Eventually your mind catches up, but then you're too old with nothing to look forward to except dying, very often alone. This society rewards workers while it shuns those who no longer can."

Louisa tapped a few keys, then closed the laptop.

"Also, you're missing a key point."

Janiss folded her arms and waited.

"Those people in there? They want to learn. They want to be productive. Do you know how much collective experience these people have? Stories? Memories? Skills? If someone like you can teach them to get back out into the world, imagine what they could do, but the world isn't ready for them and won't accept them. Someone has to reteach them here, and I very much want your help."

Janiss had to admit to herself that it sounded amazing, but there was still one problem. "Does everyone get to enjoy the benefits, or only the ones you choose?"

"That's what we're trying to figure out, dear. No one here is paying for any of this except the Cedarcrest Foundation."

She had an answer for all of it but wasn't revealing a thing.

Perhaps sensing Janiss's frustration, Louisa smiled. "Take the rest of the week to think it over. There's a storm coming in tonight and the roads probably won't be safe tomorrow or for a few days afterward. Providing you adhere to our non-disclosure, there's no hurry. We want to have someone who loves our residents working here with us."

Janiss felt her phone vibrate. Not thinking, she plucked it from her pocket and pressed a button, then smiled at Daniel's message before she realized that she had done it in front of Louisa.

"Oh, I'm sorry! That was rude of me." Janiss

packed the phone away quickly, but Louisa waved her off.

"Your manners alone are apology enough. It's refreshing to hear someone so young say it, let alone mean it. You're a rare person, Janiss."

Janiss blushed. "Thank you." Smooth talker.

"Your boyfriend?" Louisa pried, indicating the pocket her phone disappeared into.

"Yeah," she answered absently. "No...we're friends right now. Maybe more. We'll see." Why the sudden personal interest?

"Have you known him for a while?"

"Yes. Since we were in grade school."

"Does he love you?"

"He says he does."

"Do you love him back?"

Janiss started to laugh, wondering for a moment why she was even talking about it; but saw no reason not to continue. "I don't know."

"You have doubts?"

"We're both so young..."

"And what if there's someone else out there for you? Spoken like someone who's never been hurt. Your innocence is showing, my dear."

It felt like Louisa was being hurtful. Janiss didn't like the feeling, but playing dumb seemed to be working so far. "I'm not sure I understand."

Louisa stood, walked around, and leaned on the front of her desk to address Janiss more intimately. "Is there anything he wouldn't do for you? Don't think about it; just answer. Is there?"

"No."

"Then give him more consideration. You don't realize how rare that is because you've always had it." Louisa's tone became more serious. "The world is full of handsome devils who practice saying and doing everything to perfection. Those are the tools of seducers and predators, Janiss. They close the deal quickly and feast upon your naked flesh before abandoning your empty corpse in a shallow, unmarked grave."

Janiss was certain her mouth fell open upon hearing the sudden, unexpected, and horrific description. When Louisa's thin assistant opened the door, he stood by it as if escorting Janiss out was a prearranged and a foregone conclusion.

"Did you have any other questions before you leave?" Louisa asked.

"I suppose not." Janiss took a deep breath, smiled politely, and gathered her things. It was only then she realized she had forgotten she still had Ruth's gift.

"Mrs. Newcomb?"

"Louisa will do, Janiss, and I haven't been married for a very long time."

"Sorry, but can you give this to Ruth for me?"

Louisa glanced down at the gift. "She should be up to seeing you in a week. You can give it to her yourself. I wouldn't be comfortable as the go-between who lessens the impact of such a sentimental gesture. I'm sure she's looking forward to it."

Wow, could she use a lot of unnecessary words,

Janiss thought. "Thank you, ma'am."

"Louisa," she corrected.

Janiss smiled as best as she could. "Louisa."

Timothy escorted Janiss to the elevator at the end of the hall. She considered asking him about Louisa, but he didn't look like the type to divulge secrets. Keeping her mouth closed, she rode the elevator down alone and stopped at the main desk in front of Yolanda.

"Was everything okay?" Yolanda asked.

"I think so," Janiss replied. "How long have you worked here?"

"About three years. It's the best job I've ever had, but there are some interesting things going on here most of the time."

"Such as?" Janiss pried.

Yolanda smiled. "I can't say. Why do you ask? Are you thinking of applying?"

"Louisa just offered me a job."

"Who?" Yolanda asked.

"The administrator, Ms. Newcomb."

"Oh." Yolanda looked both puzzled and surprised. "Well, enjoy your evening. There's a snowstorm coming in tonight, so don't stay out on the roads too long."

"I won't. Thank you."

Janiss walked across the lobby with all the goggle-eyed fang faces looking like they were watching her leave. Between Louisa, her creepy assistant, and the medical experimentation, she decided she might actually have enough information to have Cedarcrest investigated. When she got home, her father was going to get an earful.

Chapter 9

It was getting close to sunset, but there was no sun to be seen; the sky was fading from gray to black. The driver of a black Cadillac Escalade parked off the side of Route 5 took notice of a red Kia Soul as it passed him heading toward Glenville. He casually started his vehicle, checked for other traffic and followed.

The Kia turned into a shopping center just before the merge onto Route 33 up to the college. It was the only chain grocery store in Glenville, so either it or the sandwich shop next door was the most likely destination. The Escalade's driver turned into the other side of the lot and inched along for a moment, waiting to get a better look at the Kia's owner. He noted the Glenville State College parking sticker.

The woman who emerged was young; taller than average, but on the thin side; and pleasant-looking enough. Her clothes looked more expensive than how most locals were dressed and certainly nothing a young lady would wear for visiting a prison. He had seen enough, at least enough to ask her a carefully worded question. With luck, the answer would be all the confirmation he'd need.

It just wouldn't be so lucky for her.

The driver surveyed the parking lot; the fewer witnesses the better and he certainly didn't want to see any authorities. The young woman seemed to be looking for something in her purse, so the opportunity presented itself.

He loved this part, the first meeting. It was such a simple thing for him, practiced to perfection. No one ever saw him coming or was ever prepared for him. This was the moment he savored, before something new would be his.

After circling the outside of the lot, the driver pulled up across from the young woman at a non-threatening distance, the better for her to trust and approach him on her own. It wasn't like he was driving a windowless van or that he looked inbred. Everything about the way he presented himself was clean and professional with the air of success. Why wouldn't anyone trust him?

The driver adjusted his Wayfarer sunglasses and lowered his window.

"Excuse me? Young lady?"

She looked up, enticed by his voice. He saw how beautiful her long neck looked when she brushed her hair back. She sized up both driver and vehicle for a moment, and he could tell she instantly trusted him. The poor girl couldn't have made it easier.

Shouldering her purse as she walked up to the driver's window, she seemed eager to help. "Are you lost?"

The driver picked up his computer tablet from the passenger's seat, a prop for the ruse. "I'm looking for a place called Cedarcrest Sanctum. It's a nursing home and I have an appointment with the administrator there..."

"Louisa?" the girl foolishly confirmed.

"Is that what she's calling herself these days?"

The driver pulled his sunglasses down to look the young lady directly in the eyes. He could see her demeanor changing as it struck her that she had already said too much, suspecting the danger she was in. He delighted in being recognized for the predator he was, but he still needed to close the trap to give himself the time he needed to work.

"Get into my vehicle," he commanded her.

Her will dissolved as the words reached her ears, coupled with the compulsion of his gaze. She had become his, a plaything that would obey and indulge his every whim. She absently walked around to the passenger's side door, opened it, seated herself, and closed the door.

"Does your car have a remote?" he asked.

"Yes," she answered.

"Lock it."

She did.

"Where are you staying?"

"My Gramma's house."

The driver chuckled. "Your grandmother?"

"Yes."

"You call your grandmother 'Gramma?'"

"Yes."

He smiled. "Is the house far?"

"No."

"Does anyone else live there?"

"No."

Alone. All night at Gramma's house. Plenty of time to savor his work.

"What's your full name?" he asked.

"Janiss Annette Connelly."

"Hello, Janiss. My name is Ian. Tell me what you know about Louisa and, afterward, I promise I'll take you home."

Chapter 10

There was a knock at the door.

Louisa was looking out her office window at the seal in front of the doors below. The lights had been arranged in a specific pattern, and she enjoyed the way the shadows fell across it at night.

"Come in, Timothy."

Her thin assistant stepped inside. "He may be close."

"Show me."

Louisa met Timothy at her desk. He opened one of her laptops and began touching and swiping the touch pad until a map of the Eastern United States appeared. Several colored lines appeared over the map: route indicators and predictions.

Timothy pointed at the lines. "Local law enforcement is tracking the leads of at least three suspected serial killings, only one of which has been leaked to the press. Our information points to Ian for all three tracks. He's never been this sloppy before."

"How so?"

"A church was burned down off of Route 33 between Spencer and Glenville. The police got there before it had collapsed but too late to put it out. Victims found were all part of the same family, but authorities think it was a local mass suicide or something."

Louisa nodded. "They still don't know how the victims inside actually died, then. More lost souls." She seemed saddened by it but in no way felt responsible.

Timothy brought up more information. "What we don't know is when he'll get here. One model predicts he is taking his time, while another appears he's been doubling back. Should we alert the local authorities?"

Louisa stared at the screen, lost in thought, remembering something.

"Louisa?" Timothy repeated.

She didn't respond.

"Sarah!"

Louisa blinked at the name, recovered, then looked toward her assistant wistfully. "No. He's not hiding himself. He wants us to know he's coming. It's part of his game and we have his attention. We stick to the plan: let him think the rules are his until we change them."

"Is that why there's all the urgency with Ms. Connelly?"

Louisa nodded. "Yes. What I'm going to ask of her is nothing short of life changing. The young are blessed with the belief that they are already immortal. Who wouldn't jump at such an offer?"

"I wouldn't," Timothy commented.

"That's because you were too old even when you *were* her age. Her ideals are different. I had them once myself, so I see that in her."

"Before you met Ian."

Louisa stiffened. "Yes."

"I don't think Janiss is going to accept."

She looked surprised. "Why not?"

"Take your pick. She didn't take the check, she questioned everything you showed her and I think she's worried about the residents. Your protege is probably on her way to the police."

"We both know that's not a problem."

"Except that you have no second choice if she refuses."

"Third," Louisa corrected.

Timothy scoffed. "No alert, then?"

"Review the files, but make no contact. Arrange for false tips to mislead interested third parties."

Timothy nodded and left through the same door he had entered. Louisa went back to looking out her window at the circular seal down below.

Chapter 11

Janiss unlocked and opened the door to her Gramma's house. Behind her, Ian grinned from ear to ear almost unable to bear having to wait for his thrall to step aside so he could get past her. The moment he had enough room, he pushed in to get his first look at the living room.

"Look at this place!" he said with glee. "The land that time forgot!"

Janiss stood in one spot, her face a blank expression, while Ian ran from room to room like a child on a playground. When he got to the kitchen, he could contain himself no longer.

"Is that what I think that is? An actual cellar?"

Ian couldn't get the cellar doors open quickly enough. When he opened the second door, he shuddered. It was simply perfect.

"Oh, I know where we're spending this momentous evening, my dear." He dashed back into the living room and looked directly at Janiss. "Who owns all this?"

"My father does."

"Lucky man. Do you have any tools around here?"

"Yes."

"Where?"

"In the old garage out back."

Ian smiled and headed for the back door. He had parked his Escalade alongside the garage so it disappeared against the night unless you looked directly at it. From the road, it was invisible. The garage wasn't locked, so Ian helped himself and immediately found what he was searching for: a sledgehammer. Close by he also found a shovel and a pick – all of the things he would need.

As Ian came back into the farmhouse, he set the tools just inside the cellar and started to take off his shirt. "So your father just lets you stay out here all alone whenever you want?"

"No."

Hmm. He needed to be more specific. "Why did he let you stay here this week?"

"Daniel was supposed to be here."

"Who's Daniel?"

"My boy...friend." She looked confused for a moment.

"Still making up your mind, huh? Does he usually show up late?"

"Yes," Janiss confirmed.

"Well, half the fun of doing anything you shouldn't be doing in public is the possibility of getting caught. Is there a message on your phone?"

Janiss opened her purse, removed the phone, and looked.

"No."

Ian chuckled. "Can you even get a signal out here?"

"No."

"No worries, then." He threw his shirt and

undershirt into the cellar, then kicked off his shoes and began removing his pants. "Have a seat at the table and I'll make the place nice and cozy for us. Then we can enjoy the rest of our evening together. Say, 'That sounds wonderful.'"

"That sounds wonderful."

"Damn right, it does."

After removing the rest of his clothes and tossing them inside with the rest, Ian stepped into the frigid cellar and took up the sledgehammer. With a single swing, he broke through the back wall into the hillside and continued to demolish the wall.

"Never let it be said that I was afraid of a little hard work!"

Chapter 12

The sky was black over Glenville, and the snow was coming down thick.

Daniel had to turn around before he even got to Route 5; state police were already waving cars off the road due to treacherous conditions. Fortunately, his dorm room at Glenville State College was still open to him.

Goodwin Hall was open during the week of Thanksgiving. School facilities were in short supply, but at least he would have a warm bed for the night, could charge his phone and watch a little television. With conditions getting worse and too few salt trucks out on the road to keep up with it, there was no way he was going to get out to Sand Fork until the morning at best.

It wasn't where he wanted to be.

Daniel was amazed the coupe got up the hill with the snow thickening on the ground, but keeping good tires on his car was one of the things he didn't skimp on. The parking lot was mostly empty, and the cars there were already half buried. Grabbing his gym bag and remotely locking his car, he found several other students already camped out in front of the television in the common room.

"Didn't quite make it out of here either, huh?" the RA asked.

Daniel shook his head. "I was just passing through.

Are all the roads closed? It's Jimmy, right?"

"Yeah," Jimmy answered. "Storm's all over the news. It'll probably be open in the morning. The hunters are going to love this."

None of the people in the common room were anyone Daniel recognized, so he guessed most of them must have been underclassmen. He didn't feel like talking to anyone else anyway.

Daniel swiped his key card and went into his room, tossing the gym bag into the armoire. He tried calling Janiss on her cell phone again and, when he didn't get an answer, he tried the phone at her grandmother's house. The call couldn't be completed, so he guessed the lines were down already.

Maybe this was one of the reasons Janiss kept pushing him away. It was irresponsible of him to promise he would be there on Saturday night and show up two days later.

Daniel was determined to make it right. If he got out there early enough in the morning, breakfast in bed wouldn't be the worst apology. The sooner he got to the farmhouse in the morning, the better.

Chapter 13

Janiss stood motionless in the middle of the cellar beneath a single incandescent bulb illuminating the small room. Ian pulled the outer door into the kitchen shut and pushed the inside door closed after it.

Opposite the door, Ian had dug a large trough out of the hillside and into the floor a couple of feet deep, large enough to completely an average person. A pile of bricks and rubble was on one side of the empty grave, while a mound of dirt and the tools were on the other. On the last place where the thin concrete floor still remained intact, Ian had placed one of the kitchen table chairs and seated himself comfortably.

"It's better this way," Ian confessed. "No screaming, no crying, no begging for your life. Just us. Well, you doing what I say and me enjoying the benefits, but I am generous. Let's begin, shall we? Tell me you want me to begin."

"I want you to begin."

"Take off your sweater."

Absently, Janiss removed her sweater.

"Hand it to me."

She obeyed, and he dropped it onto the pile of his own clothes. "Now your shirt."

One by one, she removed each article of her clothing at his command. She began to tremble, not with fear but due to the bitter cold of the room. It was an involuntary response, nothing he had any dominion over. Her breath turned white as she exhaled.

Ian smiled at the sight of her. She was slight but pleasant, a runner's build, he thought. Small breasts, narrow hips – but promising. He liked that she was tall but not too tall, especially in the thighs that gave her legs a longer appearance.

"I must confess to you that I had no intention to do this. You were supposed to be a message, nothing more. Knowing that you met Louisa, however, changed things. I'm afraid you can't fully appreciate who and what she is unless you've walked that road yourself; and since it was me that put her on it, it's only fair that you have the benefit of the same experience. Tell me that I should go first."

"You should go first."

"You are a generous host, my dear," Ian said with a smile. "Come closer to me – step here – and press yourself against me."

Janiss obeyed. With Ian seated and Janiss standing, she pressed her abdomen against his side straddling his leg, putting his lips in easy reach of everything from her neck and shoulders to her midriff.

For a moment, he trembled in anticipation, then opened his fanged mouth with a hint of a snarl. He started to move toward her neck, then stopped and looked up into her vacant eyes.

"Your throat will be last. I will savor that the longest."

Ian sunk his teeth deeply into her shoulder and drew the blood gathering there. It flowed easily, filling his mouth with heat. He stopped himself in time, feeling Janiss start to reel from the loss and cradled her back with his hands.

"It takes a while," Ian explained. "Much more than a pint for someone as slight as you could cause you to fall unconscious, and I wouldn't call that fair to you. I don't want you to miss anything. Didn't I say I was generous?"

Like his teeth had elongated before, the end of a single forefinger extended, blackened, and hooked like an animal claw. He used it to scratch open his own shoulder in the exact same spot he had bitten Janiss. He pressed her lips to it as the blood began to flow.

"Drink it in," he said, cradling the back of her head while pressing it down with his hand. "Drink it all."

She obeyed.

Next he indulged in her breast and then her side, taking a little and giving a little as he went. Her hips were followed by her thighs, then a little from one calf, and he very much saved her pretty little throat for last.

Then it had been enough. He could see the change in her, the resistance to his thrall beginning. With more of his blood inside of her than her own, her body began to convulse rejecting what was happening but unable to prevent it. She squeezed her eyes shut to endure pain her fragile mind could neither comprehend nor escape. When she collapsed, he caught her and held her close as she quivered.

"It's happening, Janiss," he whispered seductively

into her ear. "This is what I did for your admirable Louisa. The two of you should have plenty to talk about should you meet again; but, for now, it's off to bed with you, young lady."

Ian gently lifted Janiss up and carried her over the shallow grave before unceremoniously dropping her into it. The moment she touched the soil, her convulsions eased and ceased. When she was finally still, he began to cover her in the loose soil from the hole until she was completely interred.

Setting Janiss's clothes aside, Ian dressed himself again, admiring his handiwork as he did so. He opened the cellar doors, removed the dining room chair and closed the doors behind him. He switched off the cellar light just before he left, allowing Janiss to die alone in the dark.

Chapter 14

The roads were clear and salted on Monday morning by the time Daniel got to the farmhouse around eight-thirty, and he was worried about Janiss. Walking around the farmhouse, there was no sign that she had spent the night. Her bags were in the room she stayed in, and the refrigerator was stocked with new groceries. Her car was missing, so maybe she went somewhere. It was weird, too, as he thought about it, that he saw a red Kia Soul similar to hers in the grocery store parking lot, but it looked like it had been there all night from the amount of snow on top of it.

New plan, he told himself. She was probably out at her nursing home again doing some kind of volunteer work, so he would save breakfast in bed for the following morning. In the meantime, he didn't think it would hurt to figure out his menu and make sure everything would turn out okay.

A fresh carton of eggs was in the fridge, along with a new package of bacon. There was a loaf of bread and a stick of real salted cream butter. It was like breakfast was calling to him.

After melting a pat of butter, Daniel started a few strips of bacon in the cast iron skillet. He let them sizzle while he beat a couple of eggs inside a coffee cup to scramble them, adding a few spices from off the rack.

Just as the bacon was getting crisp, he set the strips onto a paper towel and drained out a little of the fat. He poured the eggs into the skillet and allowed them to cook in what was left, turning down the heat a little so it didn't cook too quickly.

On a whim, he looked back inside the fridge for something to drink, anything with caffeine that wasn't coffee or sugared. He remembered that the Connellys usually put sodas and other things that didn't need refrigeration into the cellar.

Daniel opened the outer door to the cellar and flipped the switch for the inside light just as he pushed the inner door open. Before it opened wide enough to see, the light bulb hanging inside exploded – the sound of shattering glass plunged the room back into darkness. Hair, fangs and dirt lunged at him from the darkness, clawing into his flesh and dragging him back into the interior. As he fought in vain to get away, something kicked the inner door shut and slammed his back into the ground. Fangs bit deeply into his neck and shoulder, ripping into him again and again.

For a moment, Daniel felt everything go still as the thing that enveloped him drained the life from his body. He closed his eyes, felt a final breath leave his lips and was glad that Janiss was somewhere far away and safe.

Chapter 15

Janiss opened her eyes.

Was it still dark? How early was it?

The bed felt wonderful, like waking up the first morning after getting over being sick. She closed her eyes again. The smell of freshly turned soil made her remember helping her Grampa work in the garden.

Soil?

Her eyes snapped open. She was lying on her stomach with one arm behind her and the other against the bed, only it wasn't a bed. She clawed at the imagined sheets only to dig her fingers into earth.

Sitting up with a start, there was a hint of light coming through a small opening very high up on the wall. It looked familiar. Her mind raced; where had she seen that light?

The cellar. She was in the cellar?

Her eyes adjusted. She was peeking over the edge of the cellar floor into a pile of rubble stacked against a brick wall. How was she looking up over the floor unless she was beneath it? She could out make the edge of the inner cellar door looming in the dim light over her shallow grave.

Janiss knew she was in danger. How did she get there? Did someone try to bury her alive?

Hold it together, she told herself. She could worry

about what had happened and what had been done to her when she was safe.

She drew her feet up into a crouched position and then stood up. The hole was no more than two feet deep and easily escaped. Moving carefully to the door, she checked to see if she had anything in her pockets, but there were no pockets. She wasn't wearing any clothes at all!

Panic welled up again. She trembled at the thought that she might have been raped and her eyes teared up in despair.

No, she thought. She wasn't dead, but she might as well be if she gave in to this. She didn't know what was happening, but if she could get to someone, anyone, it would be okay. No one except her parents knew the farmhouse and property as well as she did. She could get away.

In spite of the fact that she felt filthy and had the urge to scrub herself clean, her body didn't feel abused. In fact, she felt well rested and charged up, even ready to run a few miles; but that was probably the adrenaline from fearing for her life. The strange calm felt wrong, but she welcomed it – even feeling a little impressed with herself for keeping it together. She promised herself a good cry later.

The inner door to the cellar opened with a simple pull. It seemed unusually easy, especially since it was often so tightly wedged closed that she would have to lean her shoulder into it from the outside. She pressed her ear to the outer door to listen into the kitchen. There was a whooshing sound from a gas heater as if she were already in the room. Why would it sound so much louder than before? Was it that quiet in the house?

Confident no one was on the other side of the door, she slowly turned the knob and gently pushed outward. The door opened quietly into a dark kitchen, illuminated by the glow of the gas heater near the back door and the dull blue numerals from the digital clock on the new stove.

It was eight 'o clock at night.

Tiptoeing out of the cellar, she carefully closed the outer door and moved to look out the windows into the back yard. Snow was everywhere. When did it snow? Under the security light by the old garage, she recognized the front end of a white Saturn coupe, Daniel's car.

Was Daniel there? Was Daniel in trouble, too?

Plates and the cast iron skillet were in the sink. What looked like it might have been bacon and eggs was clogging the drain. Why would someone cook themselves breakfast only to throw it away?

Janiss thought about the cast iron skillet for a moment. It could be a weapon if she got the drop on someone, but there were far better weapons in the kitchen. There were plenty of handles to choose from sticking out of the knife block, but the butcher knife looked the most intimidating.

There were four ways out of the kitchen: through the back door, through the bathroom beside the stove, into the hallway past the freezer toward the living room, and down the side porch out into the front yard. The problem with leaving, however, was she that wasn't wearing anything and didn't have any keys. How long would she last walking in the snow? Without a car, she was in the middle of nowhere unless a truck full of hunters happened to drive by. The thought made her cringe, but was that worse than being murdered?

The house phone was in the hallway to the living room. If she could reach it, she could call for help and hide until they arrived. The problem was not being heard and if the roads were clear enough for the sheriff or state police to send a car.

She thought of another option: the guns in the back bedroom. There was a shotgun there and a couple of handguns. The shotgun was always loaded; her Grampa and dad both insisted on it. The barrel and stock was as long as her arm and she'd never fired it, but she knew how to load it and cock it if she had to. Whoever else was in the house, did they know about the guns? Did they have them already?

The phone was the easiest option, maybe the safest.

Resisting the urge to awkwardly cover herself, she thought of how many times she had walked naked back into the bedroom to dress after showering. There also wasn't much she could cover with one hand while holding a knife in the other. The floor was solid enough and didn't creak as she crossed it, but the phone was mounted to the wall in full view of the living room if anyone was in there. Just because the house was dark didn't mean she was alone.

She glanced quickly into the doorway of the ugly pink bathroom as she sneaked past it. The tiny golden nightlight inside the bathroom reflected off of the walls to create a horrific color; but it enabled her to see that the door to the back bedroom was shut, the room where the guns were kept. It wasn't unusual: that door was always closed to give anyone using the bathroom privacy. She also knew that the floor creaked in a few places in the bathroom and if she didn't have to give herself away, she could wait.

Moving alongside the wall of family photographs, she dared a quick peek into the living room. No one was there; the glow from the monster heater coupled with the utility building security lights trickling through the window revealed an empty room. That left only two more rooms and the bathroom in that part of the house to check to see if she was really alone.

The thought that she might have been drugged and left for dead by her attackers entered into her mind. The spin that she wasn't actually dead and their mistake might have saved her life gave her confidence that she might be in the house alone and safe.

Janiss lifted the phone off the hook and pressed 911. She cradled the handset to her ear and listened; there was nothing to hear. The phone was dead. It was something that happened when it snowed, the weight on the phone lines outside pulling them down. It might have been coincidence, that no one had intentionally disabled the phone.

Replacing the phone on the hook as quietly as she

could, she looked across the living room toward the first bedroom door. It was wide open.

For a moment, Janiss stood in the doorway between the hallway and the living room, imagining what might be there. Was the effect wearing off? For some reason, she felt that the house was safe. She believed it. Did she imagine waking up in a grave dug into the cellar? Was she still asleep and dreaming?

She was hurrying across the living room when the monster heater kicked off, the tiles inside dimming with a ticking sound. The noise made her freeze, giving her time to think about it. The sound was different than the one in the kitchen. It seemed odd to her that it was the monster heater she had heard from inside the cellar and not the one in the kitchen.

At the edge of the doorway, she peeked into the bedroom. A ceramic statuette of two ducklings with a nightlight behind them cast a dim light on the wall behind, creating a hazy light to see by. The only things in the room not normally there belonged to her – suitcases, her books, and a makeup bag – but where was her coat and purse? The connecting door to the far back bedroom was open, too, and she could see that the bed was made and empty.

No one was in the house.

That didn't mean someone wasn't coming back, and she still didn't know where Daniel was.

Slipping more confidently into the back bedroom, she saw a gym bag on the floor next to Daniel's coat and shoes. It was where he always dropped them when he stayed over. Janiss tried not to think the worst.

Setting the butcher knife down on a dresser, she went to the closet. She was relieved to find the weapons still hidden there. The clips weren't inserted into the handguns. When she lifted up the shotgun, it seemed too light. Was it loaded? She checked and it was.

New plan.

Leaving the handguns behind for a moment, Janiss took the shotgun with her back to her own room and put on the first clothes she could find, along with her running shoes. She still couldn't find her purse or coat.

Keys. She needed keys for the car.

She checked Daniel's pea coat pocket; they were there. While she was happy to find them, it made her worry about Daniel even more. She could use his coat, too, since she was going outside. After putting it on, she went back to the closet and shoved the two handguns into opposite pockets of the coat, the smaller gun on the right side with the car keys. That would let her keep both hands on the shotgun.

Since the door between the back bedroom and the bathroom was shut, Janiss knew it was latched on the bathroom side. With the barrel slightly down and ready to raise, Janiss slipped back through her room, into the living room and crossed into the hallway, ready for anything. Inside the kitchen, she looked through the back windows again, looking for tracks in the snow. There were none.

The back door out of the kitchen wasn't locked, so she figured someone had definitely gone out that way.

She slowly opened it, feeling the cool air rush in through the screen door. It wasn't as cold as she supposed, even pleasant feeling. Janiss pushed the screen door open and cautiously stepped off the porch toward Daniel's car.

The full glare from the garage security light flashed in her eyes. A memory flashed in her mind.

Daniel?

She had seen him; she remembered it. Where?

The light was smashed; she smashed the bulb in its socket. She kicked the door shut when...

Daniel.

Oh no.

The memory of it came flooding back. Her holding Daniel, holding Daniel down. What had she done to Daniel?

She went back inside immediately, slammed the shotgun down onto the table and opened the cellar doors. There was something in the corner to the left of the doorway, hidden in the shadows beneath the light peeking in through the tiny window. The switch in the kitchen wasn't working, useless to power a broken bulb.

Janiss felt sick as she walked across the room and turned on the kitchen's overhead light. Enough of it found its way into the dark cellar, into the corner where Daniel's body lay.

She screamed.

His head was cocked to one side with a contorted expression of pain frozen upon his face. His shirt was ripped from one side of his neck all the way down his shoulder; the flesh beneath it was torn and mangled. His clothes were soaked with blood.

Janiss slumped to her knees. The tears wouldn't stop. They made it hard to see. She wiped them away with her hands as best she could. Next to Daniel, she could see her missing purse and clothes, the ones she had been wearing before...

That man. He asked for her help. She thought he needed help.

What did he *do* to her?

Shaking, Janiss was about to wipe her tear-soaked hands dry on the pea coat until she noticed the blood. Her hands were covered in it, front and back, everywhere she had been drying her tears.

Was she bleeding?

Janiss sprang to her feet and dashed into the bathroom. She twisted the knob on the side of the medicine cabinet mirror, turning on the florescent light. As it blinked on, she could see in her reflection that the blood was coming from her own eyes. It was her own blood.

She was crying tears of blood.

The visage disgusted and enraged her, triggering some kind of transformation. The pupils of her eyes expanded, opening so wide that the whites and color were pushed away, leaving shiny black orbs staring back. With her mouth agape, she could see that a new set of teeth had pushed down over the groove between her canines and the teeth just inside of them, like the fangs of a snake. The muscles in her face were beginning to contort into something gaunt and feral. The longer she looked at herself, the more angry she became and the more monstrous she turned. She lashed out and smashed the mirror in frustration.

Janiss looked at her right hand. Thick black talons protruded almost an inch from underneath each of her fingernails, each looking as sharp as the next. The cuts from smashing the mirror were closing, leaving bloodless scars. The blood on her hands that she had wiped from her eyes was also vanishing, absorbed into her skin like a sponge.

Pieces of the broken mirror cracked under her feet as Janiss left the bathroom and headed to the bedroom. There was another mirror there. She needed to look again, even if it was for the last time. She struggled to calm down, then turned on the light to see what looked back.

Everything appeared normal again: no blackened eyes, no fangs, no talons. Somehow, she knew she could unleash them all again with a thought, eyes suited for hunting, teeth and claws for ripping flesh.

Why?

For the blood.

She recalled the taste of it. She remembered Daniel's blood, how much she wanted it and how she had engorged herself on it.

There was only one thing, one horrible creature she could think of, that survived exclusively on blood. She had seen it in the bathroom mirror. As ridiculous, maddening, and insane as it was, it was true.

It was what she had become.

It was also impossible. How could she not be out of her mind?

All Janiss knew for sure was that she didn't want to be inside Gramma's house anymore.

She didn't want to be there ever again.

Chapter 16

Ian stood on the hillside between the pine trees, looking down toward the farmhouse. The blood around his mouth was starting to fade. One more deer would be safer that hunting season, although the fat little hunter he'd drained probably wouldn't have walked after it anyway.

This time when Janiss left the house, she seemed to have swapped the shotgun for her purse. Good; she found it, then. She marched her little self through the snow, got into her dead boyfriend's car, tried unsuccessfully to start it twice, then finally got it going. Where did she think she was going to go? To the cops to turn herself in?

Ian smiled, imagining the possibilities. He remembered when he rose and took his first victim, but he couldn't recall how long ago or where it had happened. Thinking on such things often proved a distraction, so he put it out of his mind.

Bram Stoker got a few things right in that book of his. The dead do travel fast, especially when they're running away from what they are. Whether or not to destroy yourself was the easy decision to make; the hard one was if you should hide from the world or devour it.

He considered following her, just to see where she might wind up, then decided against it. As her maker, it wouldn't do if he didn't set a good example.

"Well, if my little lady is going out tonight," he whispered, "I'd better get the housework done before she gets home."

Chapter 17

The road conditions weren't too bad, and the turn back onto Route 5 was clear at Sand Fork.

Janiss glanced into the side mirrors for any other vehicles, but had turned the rearview mirror away from her. She could see her own reflection if the light hit it a certain way, and even that was more than she wanted to deal with.

At least she was out of the murder house.

She wasn't sure what she was going to do yet. The closest state police barracks was a few miles up the road; certainly none of them would mind putting a murderous monster behind bars or a bullet into its head.

Janiss started to reconsider. What if they couldn't do it? Then what?

She drove past the barracks, seeing a single patrol car parked in the front and none of the lights on inside the building. One wouldn't be enough. So much for that idea.

Janiss considered simply driving into a wall someplace. Would a fireball be enough to kill herself? What if the car didn't explode? She looked down at the fuel gauge. Daniel still had half a tank, probably what was left from filling up on the way back to Glenville from Ripley. How much fuel did you have to have in a car's gas tank to make it explode? It suddenly seemed like more trouble than it would have been worth.

She chuckled to herself, then cringed at the thought that anything should amuse her. It was all some kind of nightmare, like those stupid horror movies that Daniel kept trying to get her to watch where some inflated cheerleader kept falling down and screaming. It seemed even sadder to her that she actually considered calling her father, as if he could whip out a credit card and fix it.

After a few curves past the state police barracks, her mobile phone chimed. She had a signal, and a message had arrived. Whether it was the familiar sound of the chime being something normal or the hope of it being any kind of positive news, Janiss jerked the car off the road at the closest place she could, threw the car into park, and fished her phone out of her purse.

There was a voice mail, a call from Daniel. She hesitated, not sure she deserved to hear him one last time and afraid of what she would hear him say, but she owed him at least that much to hear him out. She pressed the play button for the voice mail and enabled the speakerphone.

"Hey!" his cheery voice greeted her. "Just left the school, got snowed in last night. I promised steaks and I'm going to get them for tonight; but don't forget I said I'd take care of Turkey Day, too. See you for lunch and stay warm till I get there!"

Janiss held back her tears. The very thought of bleeding from her eyes sickened her.

Wait. Lunch?

She checked the date on her phone. It was Monday

night. She had lost an entire day. How did that happen?

Janiss agonized over it for a moment before realizing she had bigger problems: there was nowhere she could go.

What could anyone do? She might kill her parents on sight, just like what she had done to the only friend she might have turned to. It wasn't her fault! All she wanted was to just let someone else take responsibility and tell her what to do.

Then her phone rang in her hand.

Janiss almost dropped it. It was her default ring tone for a number she didn't know. Following the typical 304 West Virginia area code, she recognized the telephone exchange as a Glenville local number. On any other day she would have dismissed it, but it wasn't any other day. She touched the screen and answered the call.

"Hello?"

"Ms. Connelly? This is Louisa's assistant, Timothy. I apologize for interrupting your holiday. Do you have a few minutes? "

"Sure," Janiss replied, close to tears again. "Why not?"

"There were a few more things Louisa wanted to speak with you about, this week if possible." There was a pause. "Is everything all right?"

"No," she replied, her voice steadily rising in pitch, "I just woke up buried in a cellar. I've lost an entire day, and I'm scared I've lost my mind!" She couldn't believe she said it, but it felt better to say it to someone.

Louisa's voice came on, clear and authoritative.

"Do you need help, Janiss?"

"God, yes!" Janiss exclaimed before she could stop herself. "I'm sorry..."

"Stop apologizing and gather your wits, child."

'Child'? Did Louisa just scold her? If the intended effect was to snap Janiss out of her despair, it worked; but she wasn't sure what to make of it. "Okay. I'm *okay*."

"Is anyone hurt?"

"Yes..." Janiss cut herself off, fearful to say anything more.

Louisa sounded pensive but concerned. "Is anyone there with you?"

That was an odd question. Janiss peered into the darkness outside of the car. "No."

"I think it would be best if you came in to see me, Janiss."

"Should I wait until tomorrow?"

"This *instant*. Can you get here tonight?"

"I...I'm almost there now."

Louisa's tone became firm. "Come straight here. Someone will open the gate for you."

Chapter 18

As promised, the gates to Cedarcrest Sanctum opened ahead of Janiss as she arrived at the facility. Louisa was waiting at the doors with Timothy standing close by. Only Louisa walked down to meet Janiss at her vehicle.

Stepping out of her car, Janiss resisted the urge to throw her arms around Louisa for taking her in, but she wasn't sure why Louisa would agree in the first place. Janiss couldn't think of a single reason why she should even trust her, but still felt like she didn't have a choice.

"Is this your...friend's car?" Louisa asked.

The image of Daniel's corpse flashed in Janiss's mind.

"I don't know where mine is. Maybe it's still parked at the grocery store up in Glenville."

"Let me have the keys," Louisa demanded without explanation.

"To this one or my car?"

Louisa smiled with reassurance. "Both, of course. We'll collect the other one for you."

Only too happy to let anyone else take the lead, Janiss handed over the keys for the Saturn and rummaged around her purse to find the keys to her own car as well. She found them, but couldn't imagine why she would have her car's keys and not her car.

Louisa looked at Janiss sternly. "Wait here until I

come back for you. Please."

Janiss was puzzled but still nodded.

Louisa walked back and handed both sets of keys to Timothy before leaning close to his ear to whisper something in confidence. Janiss was surprised how clearly she heard it.

"Have someone collect the red one at the grocery store in town and park them both in the underground. Contact me immediately if it isn't found."

After Timothy ducked back inside, Louisa walked back down to Janiss. "Thank you for being patient. Please follow me."

Janiss obeyed, following Louisa across the circular seal to the main doors and into the lobby. The doors to the public wing to the left of lobby, normally wide open, were closed. The main desk was empty; no one was around. Unlike anytime she had been there before, every one of the white lights were red, illuminated as though some kind of alert had been issued. Where was everyone?

Either sensing her discomfort or just making conversation, Louisa offered an explanation. "We're running a drill. We do them at night when most of the residents are asleep."

"What kind of drill?" Janiss asked, feeling apprehensive.

Louisa didn't answer the question and instead pressed her finger to the sensor to open the middle elevator behind the main desk. The doors opened and Louisa stepped aside for Janiss to enter ahead of her. Once they were both inside, Louisa reached down and touched the control panel on a blank spot below the ground floor button. Something hidden illuminated and the doors closed. She never even used a key card.

They weren't going up to her office. The elevator was going down.

Louisa turned around and faced Janiss. "How are you feeling right now?"

"Frightened out of my mind." Janiss felt compelled to apologize. "I had no right to come here, but I appreciate..."

Louisa silenced her with a raised hand. The elevator stopped, but the doors they had entered the car through didn't open. Instead, a different door opened behind Janiss.

She didn't even realize that it was a door until it opened. As she turned, she saw a hallway that looked like something out of science fiction or horror: a corridor of identical doors leading to a featureless silver metallic door at the end.

Five doors lined each side of the hallway, all with knobs, while there didn't seem to be any way to open the metallic door.

"First on the left, please," Louisa instructed.

Janiss obeyed and turned the knob, half expecting an interrogation room. Instead, it opened into what resembled a fully furnished, compact studio apartment. There was a small kitchenette, appliances, a sitting area with a television, and a door to what Janiss assumed was a bathroom. It was like someone buried an RV, especially with the lack of windows. What it also lacked, however, was a bed, replaced by what looked like a flat mat on the floor where a single bed ought to be.

"Are we under the walking garden?" Janiss asked.

Louisa nodded. "Very good." She gently closed the door to the room, but there was muffled second click a moment after. "These rooms are secure, inside and out."

That sounded very sinister to Janiss. "Why?"

"So that we can have a private conversation, of course. Please sit down." Louisa indicated the sitting area and set aside some kind of remote control from the closest seat across from the one she took herself.

Janiss complied, but she still wondered what would have been wrong with using Louisa's office for all of this.

"Tell me what happened," Louisa encouraged. "Start at the beginning."

"I woke up in the cellar of my Gramma's house. Someone had dug a hole, and..." Janiss couldn't get the image of Daniel's body out of her mind, and every time she saw it, she could feel the tears forming and stopped herself.

Louisa pressed her. "Go on. What was in this hole?"

"It was like a grave, a couple feet deep. I woke up in it, naked. I think someone tried to bury me alive. I don't know if they did anything else to me or why I can't remember any of it."

Louisa didn't appear to react to the story, or else she didn't believe her. Janiss tried not to let it frustrate her.

"I found someone else in there, too. The guy I was

seeing...the one we talked about. Daniel. He...he's dead."
Janiss took a deep breath. "I think I killed him," she
added in a whisper. "I remember killing him."

"How did you do it?" Louisa leaned closer.

Janiss didn't want to believe it herself. "I bit him. I
dragged him into the cellar and...I don't know."

"Was any of him missing? An arm or finger?"

Janiss stood up and backed away, her voice
trembling. "You don't believe a word of this!" She looked
around the room. "Is that why we're in here? So I don't
hurt anyone or myself? You think I'm insane?"

Louisa turned in her seat to better address Janiss.
"Can you prove any of this?"

She shuddered. "I don't think I should do that."

Louisa stood up quickly and stepped closer with a
slight grin that made her appear very sinister. "Why not?
What will happen? Will you do something to me, too?"

"Don't do that," Janiss told Louisa, glancing at her
feet, then back into her eyes. "I don't want to hurt you."

"I don't think you will, but I would very much like
to see if you can." Another step. Louisa was almost in
arm's reach.

Janiss pressed her back against the door. "Please!
I'm warning you..."

"Don't warn me, Janiss. Do something if you think
I'll hurt you first."

When the taunts became more than she could
tolerate, Janiss ceased holding back her rage. Her pupils
opened wide and her teeth elongated. "Do you see? Do
you see what I am?"

"And why should that frighten me?" Louisa stepped in close and gently brushed Janiss's hair back over her shoulder. As she did, Louisa's pupils widened, sharp fangs sliding down to mar her smile. "It's nothing I haven't seen before."

Horrified, Janiss grasped the knob. It turned, but the door didn't open. "Let me out!"

Louisa's eyes and teeth returned to normal. She returned to the sitting area as though nothing was wrong. "Calm yourself and sit back down, child."

The label of "child" was infuriating to Janiss, and she was getting angrier. She grasped the knob and twisted it as far as it would go, allowing her rage to escalate with her frustration. The metal pins holding the mechanism began to fatigue, bend and finally broke off into her hand. A dull clunk sounded on the other side of the door as the rest of the knob fell out.

"That door is two inches thick," Louisa said with a casual tone. "High-grade steel anchored with eight pins that were set the moment I closed it. It's something like a bank vault, I'm told. You'd have an easier time digging your way out through the foot-thick concrete walls."

It was wrong, all of it. If it was all a nightmare, it was getting worse.

Janiss tried to calm herself in order to think it through. "Why are you imprisoning me?"

"You're not a prisoner."

"But you know what I am!" Janiss resisted the urge to slam the broken knob down, opting instead to set it gently on the counter top as she looked toward Louisa.

"It's what you are, or you wouldn't be in here with me."
Something horrible occurred to Janiss. "You knew. How
did you know? Was it you? Did *you* do this to me?"

"I will accept the responsibility," Louisa answered
calmly, "but no, it wasn't me. I may have placed you in
danger. I suspected your transformation because I could
hear it in your voice. It has a different quality to it now,
but you likely haven't guessed why."

It was maddening, all of it. Worse yet, it somehow
made sense – and the thought that she couldn't hurt
Louisa was inexplicably comforting.

"I am impressed with your control, Janiss. You're
taking this all very well."

Janiss couldn't hold back her tears any longer. She
didn't want to take it well. "I don't want to live like this!"
She lowered her voice when she realized she was almost
screaming. "I want to die."

"You *are* dead, Janiss. He killed you already. You
can only be destroyed, although you'll find that more
difficult now. What you should really want is to ensure
that what happened to you never happens to anyone else
ever again." Louisa seemed to be leading her.

"The same thing that happened to you?" Janiss
guessed.

"By the same son of a bitch."

Janiss watched as Louisa lowered her head and
looked wistfully at the floor, lost for a moment in a sad
memory. The corners of Louisa's eyes were starting to
bleed. Janiss had questions, but she found solace for a
moment in the older woman's grief, connecting with her.

"Is that what this place is?" Janiss asked. "A place to keep his victims so they can't hurt anyone?"

Louisa looked a little frustrated for a moment, then composed herself. "It's many things; but most of all, it's a safe place. Do you want to stay?"

"I was supposed to start student teaching in Clarksburg in January," Janiss lamented. "I was going home for Christmas and New Years. Daniel was going with me."

"You can still have a life, Janiss. You're young. For a while, you can pass yourself off as if you had never died. You'll have to make adjustments. There are so many things you need to know – and quickly."

Janiss paced. "Why would anyone do this to me?"

"The reason he's here is because I lured him here. That's why you were in danger – and it was the worst of luck that he chose you. He must have been looking for someone he thought was new here."

Lucky me, Janiss thought. Not so lucky for Daniel.

"I'm having an idea, Janiss, if you could do something for me. Consider it part of your employment, if you wish. I need you to go back to where he left you. I need you to find him again."

"Who? The one who did this to me?"

"Yes. He'll likely be waiting for you to see if you return."

"At my Gramma's farm? It's a murder house, and I'm the murderer! I'm never going back there again!"

In spite of Janiss's shouting, Louisa kept her cool and picked up the remote. She pressed a button, turning the television on with a menu selection. After selecting the Internet and clicking a bookmark, a mapping application came up. Louisa deftly entered the street address Janiss had put on the paperwork from Sunday, and an overhead picture appeared of her Gramma's house.

Louisa pointed at the farmhouse itself. "Is that the main house?"

"Yes." The picture had been taken in the summer when all the trees were full of green leaves.

"He'd be willing to stay there. It looks beautiful in an old way."

Janiss couldn't tell if she was being sarcastic or not. "Why do you want me to find him again?"

"To destroy him. Why else?"

"No, why *me*?"

Louisa smirked. "Because he doesn't want you dead. He might be willing to take you on as an apt pupil. Go to him. Tell him that you want to learn, that you want him to show you everything. He'll believe you."

Janiss made no attempt to hide her suspicions. "I'm supposed to assume you just thought this pitch up? How do I know you didn't send him after me?"

"I'm right here, so there's no need to shout." Louisa entertained the idea. "Why do you think I would do this to you?"

"I don't know, and why do you keep doing that?"

"What am I doing?"

"Answering *my* questions with *your* questions! You're like one of my professors!"

Janiss closed her eyes and took a few deep breaths. Afterward, she looked up to find Louisa watching her curiously.

"Which makes more sense?" Louisa asked. "An old rival picked you randomly for being in the wrong place at the wrong time, or that I sent him to you to turn you into a killer?"

Janiss folded her arms. "I'm thinking about it."

"Go ask him. Tell him whatever you want. If he kills you, you get your wish. If he doesn't, you can learn from him; and when we're ready, you can lure him here."

"Then what?"

"Once he's taken care of, I promise to help you in any way I can, even to help you destroy yourself if that's what you still want."

Janiss closed her eyes and shook her head. "I still feel like I'm going to wake up in my bed with Daniel sitting next me, and we'd laugh at my stupid nightmare about being turned into a vampire and killing him."

Louisa reached up and cradled Janiss's cheeks in her hands. "Listen very carefully to me. When you start thirsting, child, you're going to forget yourself. Humanity will be a dream until your nightmare is sated. You're very intelligent and you have a good heart, but if you think it will be a simple thing to stop yourself from taking easy prey, this is going to be very hard on you. Ian can teach you how to control yourself if you can convince him."

"His name is Ian?"

Louisa let go of her, ignoring the question as if offended by it before looking up into a corner of the room. There was a tiny black dot Janiss hadn't noticed before. "Timothy?"

A tiny click came from the door, causing it to fall open slightly. Louisa turned to Janiss.

"You can go back to him, or you can remain here until after he has been dealt with. I need your decision."

She didn't like the sound of either option, whether it was becoming a prisoner or sucking up to a sadist. "I'm afraid," she confessed.

"Consider what Ian might do to people who live around here. Your neighbors. The college. Does he know where your parents live?"

"That sounds like a threat."

"Everyone is threatened while he remains unchecked. If you're there with him, they have a chance; you can distract him. While he teaches you what you can do, you can remind him of his humanity."

"And what if I can't? He already destroyed mine."

Louisa seemed to sympathize. "I didn't promise this would be easy, only that I needed your help and would help you in return. Was there anyplace else you thought you could go?"

Going back sounded better than being locked up, but it wouldn't be, would it? Besides, there was always the chance she might wake up; why else would everything keep coming back to Gramma's house if it wasn't a nightmare?

Janiss nodded. "I'll do it."

"Good. Let us prepare a few things for you and we'll begin. Would you prefer to wait in my office?" Louisa held the door open for her.

Chapter 19

When the private elevator opened to the lobby behind the main desk, the red lights were still on and the room was still empty. Louisa led Janiss toward the private wing.

"So, are the red lights some kind of 'vampires are loose' alert?" Janiss asked.

"I prefer the term 'immortals.' This facility is my home and sanctuary. If my enemies come for me, I want those who work for me to remain safe."

Except for me, Janiss added in her mind.

"Why a nursing home?"

Louisa stopped and turned for a moment. "Why do you think?"

Janiss still hated that she kept doing that but was starting to understand why she did. "You knew some of them?"

"Not at all. I was fifty-two years old when I was made, and that was over a century ago. None of the residents here had been born yet."

"Then why? Nostalgia?"

"I'll let you think on it for a bit."

Louisa pushed open the doors into the private wing. The first floor was a reflection of the upper floor. All the doors were closed and the same red indicators lined the hallway. At the end of the hall past the staterooms were two elevators and a stairwell. Louisa pressed a button for the elevator door and stepped into the car, waiting for Janiss to follow.

As the elevator descended, Louisa chuckled.

"What's funny?" Janiss asked, unamused.

"You're acting like a lamb being led to slaughter."

"That's about how I feel."

Louisa pressed the stop button, causing a ringing alarm to sound. With incredible speed, she turned on Janiss and pinned her against the back of the elevator with a single hand to the throat.

"Does this suit you better?" Louisa hissed.

The transformation was instantaneous. Louisa's eyes were black, her fangs showed, and her muscles swelled. Janiss offered no resistance, not even an attempt to dislodge the clawed hand around her throat.

Louisa scowled. "Why aren't you fighting back?"

"I don't believe you're really going to hurt me," Janiss answered.

Louisa thought about it, released her grip, then relaxed and became herself. She turned and released the stop button to allow the elevator to continue on.

"You have exemplary instincts, child. Trust them if you must, but be prepared to defend yourself. *He* won't be so easy to turn with a phrase."

The elevator door opened into an underground garage. She saw her little red Kia Soul as well as Daniel's Saturn parked there next to a few other vehicles.

Timothy was waiting just outside the open doors with a tablet under one arm and holding a tall, black coffee cup in the opposite hand. The moment the aroma of the warm liquid reached her, Janiss felt every muscle in her body tense.

"This is new," she whispered under her breath, trying to make light of what she was feeling.

It wasn't just what was in the cup but who was holding the cup as well. Janiss looked toward the ground away from both Timothy and the cup. It took all of her focus and willpower not to leap from the elevator and devour him. She imagined it was what being an addict must feel like, but then she could barely think at all. She invented a simple mantra and repeated it over and over: don't move, don't look and don't kill.

Janiss stood still for so long with everyone waiting for her that the elevator door began to close. Louisa jabbed the open button before taking the cup from Timothy's hand and holding it within Janiss's reach.

"This is for you," Louisa explained. "Timothy is not."

Janiss focused on her memory of Daniel in the cellar, neither wanting to see anyone else like that nor be responsible for it, but it was barely enough to take the cup without looking at Timothy. Once the cup was in her grasp, she couldn't get it up to her mouth fast enough. It was warm blood, of course; but it might as well have been perfectly salted tomato bisque served on a cold day at some trendy bistro to a starving customer. When the cup was drained, she fumbled and dropped it; but Louisa caught it before it hit the ground.

Janiss trembled with the sensation of her body getting exactly what it craved. "Does that ever get any easier?"

"No," Louisa admitted. "You just have to get stronger."

Janiss looked up at Timothy as if to apologize, but also to find out if she was able. "I suppose if you're not a vampire, you must be a blood-sucking lawyer, right?" As she guessed, it was easier looking at food after having just fed.

"Paralegal," Timothy corrected. He indicated her car – it even looked like it had been cleaned. "Your keys are in the ignition. The tank is full. Follow the exit signs out of the parking lot."

He sounded angry about it, but she didn't care.

Janiss took a step toward Timothy to leave the elevator, expecting him to flinch; but he held his ground for a moment before stepping aside. Louisa followed her out.

"So, I'm just supposed to drive back out there and wait for this Ian to show up?"

"He's probably waiting for you."

"And I can tell him anything? Anything he asks? No secrets?"

"No secrets, Janiss, but don't expect that he will do the same for you."

Janiss opened the car door and climbed in. "How long do I have to keep this up?"

"As long as it takes, but it shouldn't be long. Keep your phone with you. I may send messages that will be waiting for you whenever you get a clear signal."

"What if he won't leave the farm?"

"He has to eat sometime. You both do. Use your best judgment and trust your instincts. Go straight there."

I'm not a lamb being led to slaughter, Janiss thought. I'm a fox being set loose onto a chicken ranch.

Janiss shut her door and fastened the seat belt. The rearview mirror looked like it had been bumped a bit out of alignment by whoever drove it in. When she attempted to adjust it, she saw Daniel's car for an instant, and someone was sitting in the driver's seat.

It looked like Daniel himself.

Maybe she really was going insane?

She turned her head and looked directly at the Saturn, finding it empty. Not wanting to appear spooked she looked the other way, seeing Louisa and Timothy waiting for her to leave as she pretended to just be checking around for traffic. Janiss felt as stupid as she must have looked. What kind of traffic would there be inside a secluded parking garage in the middle of the night?

After she started her car, Janiss took a mental inventory. She had been kidnapped off of the street, killed by a vampire and woke up buried in her Gramma's cellar. She had eaten her best friend/boyfriend and was beginning to see things on her way back to the murder house to ask her killer to show her the ropes.

She couldn't imagine how things could get much worse.

Chapter 20

Janiss wasn't more than a mile down the road before she abruptly realized she would still have to deal with Daniel's body in her Gramma's cellar. It had completely slipped her mind: the entire reason she never intended to go back.

She remembered the last time she saw Daniel, when Randy told one of them to say "I love you" and neither of them had said it. It would have felt dishonest for her to say it, and Daniel must have been afraid to after all the times she had blown him off.

Was that right? Had she really been so cold?

Daniel was her best friend. They had played together for years, even with Daniel's older brother, Eric, before he graduated, just before they started high school themselves. They told each other everything – so why did it feel like there had been a rift growing between them as they both got closer to graduating from college?

She remembered her junior prom with Daniel. They arrived together, danced a little, left early and spent hours holding one another afterward and saying nothing. A caress was followed by a touch. A light peck became an earnest kiss. Hands started to roam without protest, then clothing started to disappear. After everything had felt so perfect, everything suddenly became weird, like they had done something wrong. It felt like they were ruining each other, that they should be talking to each other about the other people they were involved with and not be involved with one another.

At least it was how *she* felt.

When Janiss said something she could tell it had hurt him, yet he kept coming back. She didn't mind him being there. She had lost count of how many times they had both tried to be closer, and she had finally been ready to give in and just go with it.

Then she become a vampire and killed him.

"Ah, that's concern I hear," she heard Daniel say. She could see him out of the corner of her eye sitting in the passenger seat. She knew he was grinning at her; he never took anything very seriously, not even their relationship.

Spooked, Janiss turned and looked. No one was there.

Taking her eyes off the road, she almost missed a turn on the hill she was ascending, a mistake that could roll her pretty little car over a hillside. She jerked the car back into the turn, managing to keep the vehicle on the single-lane road.

It wasn't real. *He* wasn't real.

"You sure you know how to drive this thing?" It sounded like he was making fun of her.

Janiss didn't look, keeping her eyes on the road. Think it through, she told herself. It was fear and guilt and whatever, mixed with an unhealthy dose of insanity.

"I thought you didn't believe in ghosts."

"Stop it!" Janiss shouted. "I can't deal with you

right now! Just go..."

She glanced again. The passenger's seat was empty. "...away."

Trying not to think of Daniel or anything else specifically, Janiss allowed herself a good cry, holding back only to keep from blinding herself. She felt better by the time she reached the house; but she knew it might start all over again once she opened the cellar doors.

As she parked her car behind the house in the usual spot to the side of the garage, Janiss noticed that the kitchen overhead light was off. She hadn't taken the time to turn it off herself, so something was already amiss. She turned the car off and locked it before marching through the snow up to the back door.

Opening the doors and flipping the light switch on, everything was clean inside. The smell of bleach and cleaning fluids filled the house. Inside the kitchen, both cellar doors were open, presumably to let it air out and dry.

Trying the switch outside the cellar door, the light came on; the bulb had been replaced. Holding her breath, she looked around the corner.

The hole was still in the floor, along with some of the debris. Every drop of blood and gore had been removed or scrubbed clean. Even the trash bags had been changed.

Daniel was gone.

If she had believed that scraping the image of him off the back of her eyelids with a knife would have worked, she would have done it already. It was like she had dreamed it all, something that didn't help the fact she was already questioning her sanity. She tried to put it out of her mind, but she knew it was the first thing she was going to ask Ian about when he finally showed up.

All evidence had been meticulously removed. The floors had been swept. Even the dishes had been done. The pieces of the shattered bathroom mirror had been cleaned up, although it would have been especially impressive if the mirror had actually been replaced. Janiss wondered if seven years of bad luck applied to the dead.

Dead. Why didn't she feel dead?

Janiss pressed her forefinger against her wrist. She had a strong pulse and felt herself breathing. Her skin didn't look any less healthy.

The stove clock read just after midnight, so it was Tuesday already. How long was she going to have to wait? Was Ian actually still around? Was Ian even his real name? Louisa had been evasive about it, as if even saying the name would bring a down a curse, and now she was just waiting for him to show up. Did Louisa even know what the hell she was talking about?

It was all pissing her off.

Janiss threw open the back door and went out into the snow.

"Listen up, you bastard!" she screamed. "I know you're out here, and if you're afraid of one little girl..."

"Bastard?" a voice said from directly behind her.

Surprised, Janiss spun around, hoping she didn't look as frightened as she felt. A man stood in the shadows where the end of the latticework-covered back porch stopped, just outside the window of the bathroom.

"I would have expected 'cocksucker' or maybe 'motherfucker' from your generation," he teased, "but I'm betting you're so sweet you wouldn't say 'shit' if your mouth was full of it."

The man stepped into the light coming from the garage. She recognized his face from inside the Escalade just before he must have taken her, but it hadn't been clear until that moment. He was tall, at least six feet, and had a strong build. He was an older man, maybe Louisa's age, but still handsome. Okay, more than handsome: ridiculously handsome. Even beautiful. The clothes he wore, however, belonged to her father, obviously stolen from her parent's room over the cellar.

"Also," he added, "I'm fairly certain my father was a married man, at least according to my mother."

Janiss folded her arms and tried to look confident. "I see you helped yourself to my parent's things. Your name is Ian?"

The man stepped forward, his hands behind his back and his stride full of confidence, both commanding and dangerous. "Will agreeing to a name make me less terrifying to you?"

Janiss stammered but held onto her anger to keep her fear in check. "I don't know. Does killing helpless women make you feel powerful?"

The man smiled warmly, the same smile she remembered from the parking lot. It made her uncomfortable that it was so practiced and trustworthy. "No. And yes, I'm Ian. I'd also like to apologize for what

I've put you through." He made a sad face. "I'm sorry."

"You're sorry?" Janiss screamed at him. "You destroyed my life! You killed..."

"Your boyfriend? I didn't do that," Ian grinned, "but I did clean up after you. You really shouldn't keep leftovers around for the authorities to find."

"What did you do with him?" Janiss forgot herself and took a step aggressively toward him.

"I gave him a proper burial in a cemetery up the road. The nice thing about fresh graves is that people rarely inventory the number of bodies beneath each headstone."

Janiss felt despicable. Daniel's parents would never know what happened unless she told them, and what would she say? She *knew* them, having grown up across the street from them.

In a more somber tone, Ian added, "I can show you where, if you want."

She scowled at him. "Don't do that. You don't get to be nice to me all of a sudden."

Ian took a suspicious step forward with a dark smile, watching her face as he drew closer. Creeped out by it again, Janiss couldn't stop herself from reacting. It seemed to delight Ian whenever he provoked a reaction from her. Determined not to seem afraid and secretly dreading his touch, she held her ground as he stood close to her.

With a quick motion, he brought up his hand as if he intended to grab her hair or shoulder, amused by the way she flinched when he stopped an inch away.

Embarrassed, she actually hit him; but it was more of a slap.

"That's it?" Ian asked with mock surprise. "You hit like a girl."

Janiss was never quick to anger, spending most of her life brushing off insults and turning the other cheek. Since waking up in a shallow grave in the cellar, she was no longer feeling the need to hold back when she could just as easily lash out.

The muscles in her hand and arm tensed as her talons pushed out from her fingertips. Her right-handed attack was clumsy and easily evaded, but Ian seemed impressed by it.

"The kitten finds her claws!" he laughed. "Too bad she..."

Janiss countered with her other hand, striking Ian across his face mid-taunt. Four parallel cuts bled down his face, but the blood seemed to disappear just as quickly. The successful hit made Janiss bristle with confidence. Maybe Louisa was wrong about Ian.

"I'm ambidextrous," Janiss said with pride.

"And you've pissed me off," Ian replied.

Janiss never saw his hand connect with her. Something struck her abdomen and sent her flying across the yard into the garage doors. Reeling from the hit and amazed she could still stand back up, Ian caught up to her by the time she could raise her head to see where he was. He pinned her against the impacted door by her neck with a single powerful hand.

"What is it with all of you and this neck thing?"

Janiss managed to choke out.

"Every creature instinctively knows to fear whatever has it by the throat." His face was contorted, thick muscles bulging so much she thought his face might split apart. The cheek wound she had inflicted had already faded. "Was this Louisa's idea? Make me destroy you since I'm the one who made you?"

"She wanted you to teach me. Show me what I needed to know."

It was Ian's turn to flinch. His face softened and his grip eased. Releasing her neck, Ian put his hand reassuringly on her shoulder. Janiss still didn't like him touching her, but it was better than having her throat crushed.

"She said that?"

Janiss nodded. "God, you're fast," she said, then realized she hadn't meant to say that out loud. She pressed her hand against her abdomen, wondering if he had crushed it. It felt like something was broken. Even as she was feeling it, it seemed to be tightening again and correcting itself. It wasn't pain she was feeling after a moment. It was more like the memory of the attack itself, as though her flesh could remember the impact, but was quickly forgetting it.

Ian eyed her suspiciously. "I'm supposed to think this isn't some halfhearted plan to lure me into a trap?"

"She *is* planning to destroy you. I'm supposed to keep you occupied, remind you of your humanity. She told me to tell you that, that it wasn't a secret."

Ian looked impressed. "She's created her own game

and invented the rules. That's clever – and the only way to figure out how it all ends is to play. Am I right?"

"Are there a lot of us?" Janiss asked.

"*That's* your first question? How grand is the vampire nation? Kids!" Ian threw up his hands and walked back to the house.

"Wait!" Janiss ran to catch up with him. "What's wrong with that question?"

Ian shoved the door open into the kitchen and sat down at the table. "Do you have anything to drink around here?"

Janiss was taken aback by the question as she shut the door behind her. What would he want to drink? "Blood?"

"Bourbon," Ian replied. "Or Scotch. Whiskey! Doesn't your old man have any booze in the house? There wasn't any upstairs."

Upstairs. Janiss failed to look upstairs earlier, but she never went up there and it was usually locked. It was a tiny addition built over the cellar walls, essentially her parent's room. Seeing him in her father's clothes bothered her. It wasn't that she couldn't tell the difference, but it messed with her – as if she'd been adopted and Ian had become her abusive stepfather.

Janiss shrugged. "If there is any, I don't know where it is. Can we get drunk?"

"*Vampires* can't get drunk, but they can enjoy the taste and remember being fucked up by it. What's with all the 'we' stuff, like you're suddenly on board with the being a blood-sucking immortal?"

"It can't be undone, can it?"

"No. You're dead. You died."

"Then why wouldn't I want to know more about what I am?"

"I would have thought," Ian countered, "you would be more concerned with whether or not I raped you."

Janiss tried to hide her disgust, but couldn't pass up the question. "Did you?"

"No," Ian answered. "Your virginity is safe for all eternity."

"I wasn't a virgin. I'm *not* a virgin."

"Really? Who?"

"Who what?"

"Who took it?"

"Why do you care?"

"'*Quid pro quo*, Clarice. '" Ian was putting on some kind of accent.

"I don't know what you're getting at."

"*Silence of the Lambs.*"

"I've never read it."

Ian looked astonished. "Didn't you see the movie?"

"I'm not into horror. I really don't watch movies."

"It's not horror, exactly." Ian looked like he was thinking it through. "What's wrong with you? You're not a bookworm, are you? That box of romance novels is yours?"

"*Mystery* novels," she corrected.

Janiss couldn't understand why Ian was getting so personal. He was all over the place, changing subjects like someone with ADHD. At least he still wasn't talking about her sex life.

"It was the kid, wasn't it?" Ian asked.

"Huh?"

"Who deflowered you. Made you a woman. Agreed to bump uglies."

"You're disgusting. Why is that so important to you?"

"You act like a shut in, but you were pretty upset when you woke up and found the kid dead."

"Daniel," Janiss corrected. "His name was Daniel."

Ian beamed. "There she is! That's what you need to hold onto, Janiss. Or do you prefer Annette? I always liked that name, like Annette Funicello."

Janiss looked confused. "I don't know who that is."

"The Mouseketeer. She had...you know what? Never mind. Back to this 'Daniel.' Did you sleep with him?"

Janiss shook her head slowly. "You're impossible. You're like a crazy person."

Ian snapped his fingers. "*V for Vendetta*, right?"

"What's the quickest way I can kill myself?"

The question blindsided him, but he recovered quickly. "Seriously? Right now?"

He seemed to think it was all a joke, and Janiss was deathly serious. "If you're not going to help me and Louisa's not going to help, then I'll just walk out into the sun at dawn and explode or something."

"That only happens in the movies. In what chemistry or biology class did they teach you that cadavers explode in sunlight? And didn't you say you don't watch movies?"

Janiss rolled her eyes. Movies were Daniel's thing, especially the horror flicks. Dream stalkers, maniacs, cannibals – any stupid monster that chased and killed normal people, Daniel loved it. If anyone loved anyone else or, God forbid, actually consummated a relationship, their swift and horrific demise was assured.

"Daniel used to try and make me watch them, including a couple of vampire films."

"You know who screwed them up, right? It wasn't that *Twilight* broad. It was Frank Langella. 1979. Ruined it for everyone."

Janiss didn't respond. Her eyes started to bleed.

"*Now* you're going to cry?"

"Can you focus for one minute?" Janiss pleaded. "I don't know all this movie stuff and I don't want to hurt anyone. I don't want to die or be destroyed or whatever you call it; but if it means no one else is killed by me, I'll do it. I didn't ask for this and I don't want to be responsible for it. Yes, I slept with Daniel – more than once if it's so goddamned important to you – and it was nice; but he wanted to get serious and I wanted to graduate."

"How's that working out for you?"

"Fuck off!"

Janiss expected him to continue taunting her, but Ian's demeanor changed instead. He leaned back in his chair, folded his arms and sized Janiss up.

"Okay," he said simply.

"Okay what?" She was already defensive.

"I'll help you. I'll tell you what you want to know."

Janiss was sure it was just another one of his games but was hopeful. "Not a joke?"

"Stake my heart and hope to die." He made a stabbing motion toward his chest.

Ian was still being foolish, but Janiss thought she could see the change. She got that he had been provoking her, but she held out hope that she might actually have a normal conversation with him. She only wished she didn't feel so foolish for needing to trust him.

"And no more movie references?"

Ian grinned. "As you wish."

Chapter 21

The silver-metallic door at the end of the hallway opened downward, descending until it fell completely flush to the floor with a clang. Timothy stepped into the interior of what Louisa called her "training room."

The circular room was twenty feet in diameter, with two additional doors spaced an equal distance from the others. The walls between them were tiled with the one-foot square, stone Aztec face masks: the same design used on all the walls in the main lobby and set into the seal in front of the facility. Above the room, a dome ceiling lit from the circumference created an eerie light. The dome was enhanced by intricate designs made to look like cut stone and matched to the wall. The floor below was seamless black stone, polished so that everything above it was reflected.

Timothy thought of it as a tomb. All it was missing was a spherical boulder to chase archeologists out.

In the center of the room was Louisa. She was seated on a carpeted mat with her legs crossed underneath her, wearing a dark purple *gi* like a meditating marital arts master. Her silver-blonde hair was braided into a single plait down her back. In front of her were two black batons, deliberately arranged and in easy reach.

Ignoring the intrusion, she continued to manipulate a touch-screen computer tablet. After setting it on the floor in front of her, Louisa closed her eyes and resumed her meditation.

"That door was closed for a reason, Timothy."

"Since you insisted on having no speakers on the inside of a soundproof room, opening the door is the only way to get your attention."

"That was also for a reason."

A burst of compressed air from one of the stone faces sent a ten-inch long wooden dart hurtling across the room toward Louisa's heart, just missing Timothy's arm. She brought her hand up in time to intercept it, catching it cleanly with her eyes still shut.

It unnerved him, and he knew she meant for it to.

"Is Ian on his way here?" she asked.

"No," Timothy answered.

Louisa opened her eyes and glared at him. "Then why am I being disturbed?"

As Timothy stepped out of the doorway, the door rose up just as quickly and clanged closed.

"I'm concerned about Janiss."

"What of her?"

"You sent a dangerous young woman without any guidance back to the rogue who turned her into a killer."

Louisa set the dart on the ground and reached for her tablet. "You have grasped the situation succinctly, as always." Her tone was dismissive.

"We're ready *now*. Phase Three has been sitting idle for months."

She looked puzzled as she swiped at the tablet. "Don't you see what an opportunity this is?"

"I believe that is the source of my complaint. We both know you intended to groom Janiss as your replacement, offering to make her like yourself. By sending her back to your mortal enemy, you risk strengthening his position."

"It weakens his position. She's a distraction to him, whether he plays along or amuses himself taunting her. She may or may not learn something that I never did."

"He might destroy her. You could have saved her."

Louisa looked pensive as she set the tablet down and folded her arms. "Don't think for a moment I believe she is expendable, but you don't know him like *I* do. If he meant to kill her as a message, he would have done so and thrown what was left over the gate. Instead, he turned her; so he must want to see what she'll become. It was her innocence that attracted him; but it was her potential that kept her alive, in a manner of speaking."

Timothy didn't budge. "What if he allies her to his position?"

She grinned. "It's not a master-child thing like those programs you watch. You know that anyone of the blood cannot be enthralled, so her will is her own. He can't make her do anything."

"He can manipulate her. You know he will."

"It doesn't matter," she said with a raised voice. "The point is to keep him occupied. I will deal with the aftermath once the task is complete."

"Isn't the entire point of Phase Three that you won't be doing anything afterward? Then it will fall to me."

Louisa conceded the point. "You can make whatever decision you wish when the time comes. Until then, I prefer not to be questioned in this."

That was happening more lately as Ian drew closer, Louisa tightening the reigns at Cedarcrest. Timothy didn't know why exactly, but he hoped it wasn't because she was second guessing herself out of fear.

He nodded and started to leave before when he heard Louisa ask him another question.

"I'm curious, Timothy. Why any concern for Janiss at all? You don't know her other than what we've researched. What has gotten to you about her?"

Timothy turned back to faced her. "She seemed so full of life when she was here before, so full of fire. I think something precious may have been lost when she was made."

Louisa smiled warmly. "She reminds me of someone else I met once, this poor little husk of a man who came to my home. He was a diligent student with little more than his career on his mind, as if it could replace everything else missing in his life."

"I think I remember him." Timothy looked off absently. "You had no idea he'd given blood a few hours earlier, and you panicked when he collapsed. I think the mistake you made was ending your thrall before you revived him."

"And he wasn't afraid, was he?"

"He should have been," Timothy replied, preferring to think of himself as someone different back then. "You could have killed him easily enough – or simply made him forget you."

It had been over a decade ago. He was a student at Alderson-Broaddus College in Philippi, West Virginia, studying business administration and pre-law. After he let a co-ed talk him into participating in a blood drive that day, he dropped off a book and some papers to an old Colonial home as a favor to his history professor. The owner turned out to be Louisa. She invited him in with the intention of only taking a little from him, not knowing a little was still too much. He awoke the next morning in her care and saw her for what she was. His curiosity outweighed his fear and they became friends.

"I think he and I shared a similar loneliness," Louisa added. "We needed each other then, he and I."

"And now?"

She spoke very softly. "I don't know what I'd do without him."

Timothy dared to look smug at her admission. "Then why would you dismiss him so readily in this if you trust him in all other things? Why force this on Janiss?"

"When something hurts you, you learn to fear it. The longer you take to confront that fear, the more it grows. Before long, a day will come when you can't even imagine stepping foot out of your own front door..."

Timothy could hear the regret in her tone. He empathized with her, understanding all too well she had built a prison for herself at Cedarcrest, thought he had helped her to give it a more important purpose. Still, her point was clear.

"You want her to face her demon," he clarified. "*Your* demon."

She smiled wistfully at his emphasis. "Don't discount her inner strength, my friend. Something needs to kindle her flame. Her fire already burns very brightly, or else neither Ian nor I would have been drawn to it."

"It's still a terrible risk."

"I know, but if she can't overcome this, how can we expect her to do what we'll ask of her? Think of what she could be."

He knew one answer, of course: Janiss wouldn't have to spend the next century fearing Ian the way Louisa had. They would see to that.

Timothy took a last look around the inside of the room. "Has it ever occurred to you that, with no one else around, you might be trapped here in agony for hours after making a single mistake?"

"Yes. It's called incentive. Risk brings reward." Louisa smiled pleasantly at him before reaching for her tablet again. "Now, get out before you get hurt."

It was over a decade too late for that, Timothy thought as he exited.

Chapter 22

Locust Knob.

Janiss recognized the location the moment Ian had described to her where he had buried Daniel. She had family buried there already, including her grandparents, but she wasn't sure Ian knew that. The mountaintop cemetery was next to a one-room church that had closed shortly after her grandparents had passed away.

Behind the wheel of her Kia, Janiss expertly navigated the blacktop roads through the night. Most of the roads were single-lane or had no markings at all, and many of the homes along the way were either abandoned or empty. The few that did have lights on were for hunting groups; they even passed a bonfire along the way.

"You should have seen this countryside a hundred years ago," Ian said with a casual tone.

Janiss didn't know that he was from around Gilmer County. She had just assumed he was there for Louisa. "Did you used to live around here?"

Ian turned toward her and flashed a knowing smile but added nothing more. He was teasing her and being intentionally evasive, so she thought she would ask something more specific.

"You mentioned movies when I asked about walking into the sunlight at dawn. I thought vampires were afraid of sunlight."

Ian sighed. "It's not our cycle. It can't kill you, but it makes you vulnerable."

"How?"

"It's...hard to explain."

Janiss was already tired of him dodging questions. "Try."

Ian waved her off with a dismissing expression, then went back to looking out the window.

"Do I have to say please? Are you going to make me beg for every answer?"

Janiss hadn't realized that when Louisa asked her to keep Ian occupied that it was going to be a babysitting job. Worse yet, it wasn't like she could keep Ian from misbehaving, either; the only thing she could do was distract him. He'd already demonstrated that he was stronger and faster than her, and whether he was actually sane or not was still in question.

At the top of the hill, the headlights reflected off of an old white church with peeling paint. A sign high up on the side of the building was painted with green letters: Church of Christ, Locust Knob, house built 1893, elevation 1215.

"This is it," Ian confirmed.

Janiss parked the car. No sooner had she put the gearshift in park, Ian reached over, turned off the key, and plucked the fob from the ignition before she could take her hand off the shifter. He got out and slammed the door behind him as Janiss got out.

"Why do you want my keys?" she asked.

"Nothing. I just don't want you to drive off

without me." His tone was smug and triumphant.

Janiss put his foolishness out of her mind and caught up to him on the other side of the church in the cemetery. Her memories of the place were from when her Gramma and Grampa used to take her there for church on Sundays in the summertime. It had been years since she had been up there, but she still knew the way by heart.

"There." Ian pointed out a fresh grave.

Janiss hadn't realized they still used the graveyard. The temporary name placard read "Abe Massey," but he was no one she knew. There wasn't even a headstone yet.

She imagined herself buried beneath the heaped dirt pile, wondering what her own parents would think if she never came home again. The moment she thought it, she wished she hadn't. Everyone she knew was a phone call away and she couldn't say a word to any of them.

"We can't leave him here."

Ian disagreed. "Sure we can. He's already in there and we didn't bring a pick or shovel."

"He has family up in Ohio, friends of my family. They're going to want to know what happened to their youngest son."

"Think about it, Janiss. Your house might be clean, but you can't get evidence off of a corpse unless you destroy it. They'll know where he was. They'll know when he was there." He made sure he was in Janiss's line of sight. "They'll know it was *you*."

"So all vampires have to learn how to cover up murders?"

"Or start watching 'Forensic Files.' Oh, and never take out an insurance policy on your victim. Dead giveaway every time." He stopped himself from laughing at his own pun.

Janiss scowled. "I thought we agreed on no more movie references."

"That was a television reference. Of *course* you have to learn how to conceal a murder! How else are you going to feed yourself?"

She thought about it. "Can't I just feed off of another vampire?"

"Like Louisa? By the way, did she feed you before you left?"

"Yes."

"With what?"

"Warm blood... in a black coffee cup..."

"Right. Was it her blood?"

"I...guess." She had no idea.

"How big or tall was the cup?"

Janiss gestured with her hands on the approximate size.

"So, a tall one. Two-to-three cups, or a pint to a pint and a half. That's enough to cause most humans to pass out."

"Even a vampire?"

"Vampire blood won't sustain you. That's why you don't crave it. Neither will animal blood and certainly not rats. We feed on the living, on human beings. There are no convenient shortcuts so writers can have their undead characters going to high school. Who gave you the blood?"

"Her assistant, Timothy."

Ian flashed an evil smile. "Smelled good, didn't he?"

Janiss felt disgusted at the thought, but Ian was driving at something even though he was dragging it out.

It was the first time she had thought about it. Recognizing the smell of blood, yes, that was new; but *everything* had a different scent about it, an individual quality that was more precise than before. In spite of that, neither Louisa nor Ian stood out to her the way Timothy had.

"If he could still hand it to you," Ian added, "chances are it wasn't his."

"They have medical facilities there. They probably had the blood stored..."

"Vampirism isn't a disease. You're a mystically animated corpse that imitates the living so you can feed off of it. You can't freeze or dose vital humors, what you call blood. It has to be fresh, less than an hour once it's drawn, but always best off the tap. Where else would Louisa get fresh blood that wasn't her own or wasn't freshly squeezed out of her manservant?"

Janiss had already considered it, but dismissed the idea since she wanted to trust Louisa. "The residents? Ruth?"

Ian smiled. "There! A nice, warm cup of Ruth. How was she?"

Oh God.

Louisa had said she would let Janiss think about it

for a bit, but the subject never came up again. Maybe it wasn't Ruth. Vivian? Mr. Fisher? All of them?

"We're all monsters," Janiss whispered in defeat.

"See? Now we're making progress." He leaned closer to her ear. "Don't be ashamed of what you are. It isn't evil; it's enviable."

She jerked away from him. "I need some time with this, Ian."

"We have all of eternity." He made a grand sweeping gesture. He was like a spoiled child that always got his way.

"No, I mean...can you go away for an hour and come back? I'm asking for some time alone."

"Oh. Alone. Okay. At least an hour, right?"

"I'd appreciate it."

Ian grinned. "How much?"

Janiss didn't answer him, refusing to play his game.

"Fine. I'll be back." He chuckled at himself again, then walked away into the darkness.

Janiss's plan was a simple one: wait for a while until Ian was out of earshot, then call Timothy and find out where the blood came from.

Chapter 23

The phone rang. Timothy opened his eyes, glanced at the phone, and saw it was Janiss. Before the third ring, he had sat up in bed, composed himself, and answered.

"Cedarcrest Foundation..."

"It's Janiss Connelly. Put Louisa on the phone." She sounded furious.

"That's not possible at this time. She's indisposed at the moment."

"Doing what? Feeding off of the elderly? Who's blood did you give me?"

Uh oh.

Timothy hadn't discussed with Louisa what they were going to tell Janiss about that, so he didn't answer right away.

"If you're thinking about what lie you're going tell me," Janiss continued, "I promise I'll come up there tomorrow night and try to pull your intestines out through your throat."

"Ms. Connelly..."

"You're going all customer service on me now? Whose blood was it?"

Timothy didn't like being talked over, especially by someone who didn't really know him, but he intended to remain cordial. "I'm trying to help you, Janiss. I may be the only one who is."

The line went quiet for a moment.

Janiss spoke more softly. "Back in the parking garage, when you sounded so angry? You were mad at Louisa for sending me back, weren't you?"

Very astute, he thought. "Yes."

"Fair enough. Tell me where the blood came from. Please." Her tone was calm but worried. It couldn't hurt to tell her the truth.

"Five different donors. They are all aware of what Louisa is. They donate willingly."

"Willingly? In exchange for a glorified hotel room?"

"In exchange for *her* blood."

Janiss went quiet again.

"Are you still there, Janiss?"

"Yeah. Are you going to be in trouble for telling me this?"

He flinched at the question. "No more than usual." She actually sounded concerned for his wellbeing, and he couldn't imagine why. "Where are you right now that you have a signal?"

"On a mountaintop. In a cemetery next to a church."

"Listen to me. You have to go to ground before the sun rises."

"All right," Janiss said. "What happens if I don't?"

"Louisa calls it *corpus visage*. Your abilities are greatly diminished in the daytime. It won't kill you, but it reveals you while you're in a weakened state: all the signs of being dead, especially in direct sunlight. It makes you vulnerable. Being in the ground and staying in contact with it suspends you, even your need to feed."

"How long can I stay like that?"

"Louisa suggested some vampires can spend years or decades like that."

"Is there anything else you can tell me?"

"Louisa doesn't share all of her secrets. Are you sure you can go through with this?"

"I don't know. He...he's all over the place. Temperamental and insane, yes, but...I'm trying to hold it together in front of him, but I'm afraid of what he'll do."

"Please be careful."

"I will. Thanks, Timothy. Let me know if you need anything from me. I appreciate this."

He didn't know what to say. "You're welcome," was all he could come up with. "And Janiss?"

"Hmm?"

"Louisa is ready for Ian *now*. She seems to think that you delaying him will give her some added advantage. You don't have to risk yourself unnecessarily. I'm also very sorry this happened to you."

"Yeah," she replied with a somber tone. "Me, too."

The line clicked off.

Chapter 24

Hours.

Ian had been gone for hours and it was getting brighter outside. On the flat of the mountaintop, she was looking across at the horizon in every direction. Unless she was inside the church or in its shadow, she would be exposed to the sunlight the moment it rose. Although the cold remained, the early winter storm was over and the cloud cover was gone. The black starry sky was turning an intense blue on the eastern horizon.

The brightening sky worried her, especially since she didn't know exactly what would happen to her at sunrise. The tree-covered hills at the farmhouse were so high you might not see the sun before ten in the morning on a clear day, and even then it would disappear before three in the afternoon.

Janiss checked the clock on her phone. It was seven exactly. She also noticed her phone's battery was almost dead. Small wonder since it hadn't been charged since Sunday.

Where the hell was Ian?

Janiss weighed her options. Timothy said she needed to go to ground, and she remembered how deep the hole in the cellar was. The cemetery was out of the question since the ground was frozen. She didn't have any tools, and the only recently disturbed grave had two occupants already. The thought of intentionally burying herself wasn't a happy thought, but she had already heard enough to suspect she didn't want to know what it would be like staying up past her "dead time."

"Ready for a dirt nap?" she heard Ian call out to her as he came hiking up over the hillside.

"I guess I don't have to ask if you're doing this on purpose, do I?"

Ian flashed that despicable smile again. "Waiting until the last minute? Why would you think something like that? Did you get enough alone time?"

"What's going to happen to us if the sun comes up and we're still standing out here?"

"Let's not find out." He tossed her the keys.

As she caught them, the sound of a vehicle speeding up the road drew their attention. They couldn't even see it yet.

"It's a cop."

"How do you know?"

"He was driving around earlier. Looked like he was looking for someone."

Janiss panicked. "Daniel?"

"No one knows he's missing. They're probably looking for poachers."

"If we're not doing anything wrong," Janiss suggested, "let's just go."

Ian chuckled. "Because people who rush off when the police arrive don't look suspicious at all, right?"

Janiss pocketed her car keys and waited. A black and white Ford police interceptor appeared at the top of the hill with the words "Gilmer County Sheriff" emblazoned on the side. The officer parked next to Janiss's Kia, left the vehicle running, and got out. He looked older than Ian and seemed relaxed.

The officer stepped up and nodded at them both. "Mornin', folks. Been up here long?"

"No, sir," Ian answered. He pulled her into a family-familiar embrace and Janiss tried her best not to wince. "My niece and I were just waiting to watch the sunrise and visiting some relatives, then thinking about a little breakfast."

"Uncle Ian" looked toward Janiss and nodded in the direction of the officer. Was he implying him as the aforementioned breakfast? Janiss responded with a warning glance, dreading that she couldn't stop Ian if she tried. This was exactly what Louisa had sent her for, but what could she do about it?

It also didn't help that the policeman smelled so good, either. How was she already thirsty again? Louisa had warned her that needing to feed didn't get any easier.

The officer nodded as if to approve the plausible explanation. "Seen anyone else up this way? A green-and-white Chevy truck with a couple hunters? We received a tip that they were hunting before sunrise on private property."

"Well, the signs are clearly posted around here. We haven't seen anyone else, have we, dear?"

Janiss wriggled out of Ian's impromptu hug but reluctantly played along. "No."

Looking back at the officer, she imagined tearing

into his neck. She would gratefully hold the man down for Ian to go first as long as she got her share and she hated herself for knowing it. She couldn't believe how aggressive she felt just standing near him.

At that instant, the sun rose.

As the first rays of golden light appeared, it felt like something reached into Janiss's chest cavity and hollowed her out, like being embalmed for a year and then able to feel again. Her heart seized and stopped before her breathing ceased. Her hands deteriorated as she looked at them, as if her beauty was an illusion. She was turning into a corpse in full view of the officer and couldn't stop it. Her strength was fading and it was getting hard to even stand.

With a desperate expression, Janiss looked toward Ian for guidance; but he was looking even worse. Bone was showing through his jaw and almost no flesh remained to hold his left eye in its socket. His hair had become thin and white, and he was looking more horrific by the second.

Ian continued his conversation with the officer as though nothing was amiss, but she noticed how slowly and deliberately he started to speak to the policeman.

"Tell me about your plans for Thanksgiving," Ian said. "Do you have a lot of relatives coming in?"

It was a living nightmare. Both of them were rotting away in the sun while the officer stood by and watched! How was he oblivious to it?

The only good thing about how she felt is that it completely distracted her from her thirst. All she wanted to do was crawl into a hole and be dead, and the one in her cellar sounded perfect.

"Ian, please take me to the house," Janiss whispered, starting to fall over.

Ian caught her. "What's your name, officer?"

"Earnest Strickland," the man answered without hesitation.

"My niece is feeling a little under the weather, Earnest. I'm going to take her home. It's pretty treacherous on these roads at night, so I think your poachers might have lost control and crashed down the hillside someplace. You'll probably be busy taking care of that today, right?"

"Yes, sir," Officer Strickland answered.

"Does your patrol car have a dash cam?"

"Yes, sir."

"Is it on right now?"

"It's been broken for about a month. Waiting on an appropriation to get it replaced."

"I hope you get it soon. Happy Thanksgiving to you."

"And to you."

As the officer got back into his vehicle, Ian helped Janiss into the passenger's seat of her car and took the keys out of her pocket. After the officer left heading in the opposite direction, Ian drove Janiss's car over the back roads as fast as he could while Janiss sat perfectly still, suffering in silence.

"It gets more tolerable as you age," he explained to her, "but you can't pass out from the pain. That's the bad part, but you'll feel better again once you go to ground. In fact, once you hit the dirt, you won't feel a thing."

Janiss remembered having more questions, but couldn't think of them to ask. Every moment on the road felt like an eternity, every second crawling by as she suffered. She even tried to make herself angry to offset it, but nothing helped except holding completely still.

It was debilitating. She imagined being in one of the Cedarcrest hospice rooms, wasting away to nothing as everything hurt but nothing would work. It horrified her, the thought of waiting to die – actually *wanting* to and not being able.

Ian parked her car in the back and scooped her up into his arms. He kicked the back door open and fought his way through the doors to get her into the cellar. Once inside, he removed her coat and ripped her shirt off before laying her back first into the shallow grave, then continued to undress her.

The more of her flesh that came in contact with the earth, the less pain she felt until she felt nothing at all. Her eyes closed and the tranquil darkness embraced her.

Chapter 25

"Good eee-vening," Ian said with a cartoonish accent as Janiss poked her head out of the cellar. He was reading the local newspaper, *The Glenville Democrat*, the one that used to be delivered all the time when Janiss's grandparents were alive. Seeing Ian wearing her dad's clothes and denim jacket with the newspaper open, everything felt familiar for just a moment.

Ian was a conundrum.

He had killed her first before setting her up to kill Daniel, yet he seemed perfectly willing to take her under his wing. When she almost collapsed at sunrise, he brought her home and put her in the ground, which sounded horrible in just about any other context. Was he toying with her emotions on purpose, or was there something decent about him underneath all the bravado and foolishness?

Then she noticed the decanter filled with blood on the table. Janiss surprised herself by not chugging it down the moment she saw it, but she recognized it as the aroma that woke her up. It was right there and so very tempting.

Ian turned one of the pages. "I won't answer a single question until that is gone." He pointed at the decanter without looking at it. "I hope you like the clothes I set out for you."

"They're all right. Is that yours?" she asked. "The blood."

"That sounded like a question." He turned another page.

Janiss sat down at the kitchen table in front of the decanter. The container was for wine, not blood, but it wasn't hard to imagine that it might be something else inside. The thought of drinking it felt wrong, but her craving for it justified any excuse that popped into her head.

I'll sip it, she told herself. Just a little at a time.

She gulped the entire contents down the moment it touched her lips. Ian made no comment or gesture either way, engrossed in some news article or comic strip. Embarrassed for herself and certain Ian was secretly laughing at her, she took the decanter to the sink, washed and dried it, then replaced it on the shelf above the microwave.

"I'm going to take a shower and wash my hair," she told Ian, as if it were merely a point of information.

"We have some yard work to do first." Ian closed the newspaper and folded it smaller before setting it aside. "You'll definitely want a shower after that."

Janiss looked at the time. It was after six in the evening.

"Yeah, you slept in. Sunset was after five. Did we learn anything this morning?"

"Don't miss bedtime." Janiss remembered the pain and felt completely defeated.

Ian perked up. "Hey, don't be like that. You're

doing great!" For an instant, he sounded amiable, but she knew it wouldn't last long.

"Whose blood did I just drink?" she demanded.

"To answer your original question, it's not mine. We can't feed one another, remember?"

Janiss looked out the kitchen windows again, then back to Ian. "You seem to get along just fine around humans. Why can't I do that?"

"You have to learn to out-think your instinct. Fill up before you go out, or promise yourself something later to pass up easy prey."

It made sense to her. Janiss was able to look Timothy in the eye after she drained her cup; but if she hadn't, Louisa would have had to stop her from attacking him. Or worse, Louisa might *not* have stopped her. Neither Ian nor Louisa seemed to play by any rules at all.

"Yesterday's lesson was entitled, 'Dirt naps are your friend.' Today's lesson is called, 'What doesn't kill you hurts like hell.'"

Oh goody, Janiss thought.

"If you want to keep those clothes in good shape, put on another shirt and some pants that you won't mind getting messed up and meet me out back."

As Ian went outside, Janiss went to her room and changed into a set of gardening clothes. Everything still felt dirty, but she couldn't be sure a shower would make her feel any cleaner. She put her phone on its charger and went out back.

The door to the garage in the back yard was open, and she could see the light on. Ian came out a moment later, stuffing something into his back pocket before he closed the doors again. When he saw Janiss wandering toward him apprehensively, the insane showman that shared his brain reared its head again.

"How about the nice officer that we met this morning, huh? Did you have any questions before we move onto the next topic in the syllabus?" Ian pretended there was a larger group of people for an audience than just Janiss, then pretended to pick her from the imaginary crowd. "You there! The pretty little thing from the cellar. What's your question, miss?"

"Why didn't he see us for what we were in the sunlight?"

"The policeman? Great question – but I'm not going to answer that until tomorrow, since today's lesson has nothing to do with it. Hold onto that one, we'll come back to it later in the semester. Anything else? Yes, you!"

"I preferred you when you weren't acting so silly, like you actually cared about something."

"That question was in the form of a statement, so no more questions this round. Please step up to the garage door and put your back against it."

She didn't like the sound of that. "Why?"

Ian grinned and stepped out of character. "This is going to be a reenactment of our epic battle last night when I pinned your little neck against the door. I'm going to show you how else that could've gone instead of you pussying out."

Janiss gritted her teeth. He was provoking her, she knew it, and she wasn't altogether against it. It felt good letting her rage seethe a bit, better than she had felt in a while.

"Fine. I was about here." She stood against the garage door with a wicked grin, daring him to make a move.

Ian nodded in approval. He took a stance, put his hand gently around her throat and pressed down just a little. "About like this?" he asked.

"I think so."

"Perfect." With blinding speed, Ian pulled the mystery object out of his back pocket and drove it into her chest, so far through that it pierced the garage door behind her, stapling her to the door.

The pain of enduring sunrise was nothing compared to the sudden impalement of a wooden stake through her heart. The effect was immediate and persistent. Ian took a step back and admired his handiwork.

"How's that feel?"

Janiss tried to scream, but she couldn't. Her voice barely came out as a whisper.

"Good!" Ian encouraged her, as if there was anything she could do but hang there. "Now, try to pull it out."

Her arms would barely move. The searing pain was too distracting. It took all of her concentration just to lift her arm, bend it at the elbow and touch the end of the stake. The moment she managed it, it hurt even worse. She let her arms fall limp. Would this destroy her? Is that what she was feeling?

"That's it?" Ian asked. "You're just giving up?"

"What else can I do?" she whispered.

Ian leaned intimately close to her ear. "Not a damn

thing. The point is that you need to protect your heart, specifically from wooden stakes. Just like sunlight won't kill you, a stake leaves you vulnerable and completely helpless. Also, since you can't get to ground and you can't pass out, the constant pain is yours to endure for as long as you like."

"Okay, I got it," Janiss whispered, wincing.

Ian didn't move. Was he enjoying her torture?

Janiss was already desperate. "Take it out," she begged him.

Ian put his finger on the end of the stake and wiggled it. Janiss flailed at his touch until he stopped.

"Please!" she cried, but she could barely hear her voice.

"I'm going to leave you here like this," Ian told her. "For about an hour. Just one hour. I know you can do this. Of course, I'm not really giving you a choice."

Janiss tried to think of anything she could say that would make him free her, but Ian seemed to react to threats better. "If you leave me here and I ever get loose, I swear to fucking God..."

Ian twisted the stake, sending her into convulsions. After they subsided, he kept his hand still on the end of the stake.

"Are you through?" he asked her without any hint of anger.

She nodded feebly.

Ian let go.

"One hour. I promise. You can do this."

Chapter 26

Janiss couldn't tell anymore how long Ian had been gone.

She tried counting at first, but lost count and couldn't bring herself to start again.

She knew why he had chosen that spot. The only way it could be seen was from the backyard. Anyone driving by in the middle of the night, who happened to look in the right direction, still wouldn't be able to see her. Even the gas company trucks that serviced the wells on the property didn't run after dark.

While Janiss couldn't see the main road, she could see the light reflected from the utility building down by the garden. Ian had gone into the house, so she assumed he was still there, probably watching a stupid movie on satellite.

So who was walking toward her up from the main road? The shambling walk was familiar.

It was Caleb.

He must have been walking up to the back door and then noticed her. Now he was coming toward her, and if Ian was watching, he would probably kill him.

Caleb stopped a few feet back and looked hard at Janiss. He seemed to be deciding what to do.

"Go," she whispered. "Run."

Caleb leaned closer. He either couldn't hear her or didn't understand her. He stared intensely at the end of the stake.

New plan, Janiss thought.

If she could get him to pull the stake out, she could get him to safety before Ian knew he was there. Of course, the whole thing could be a ruse if Ian was watching. Whatever she was supposed to do didn't matter; she would try to save Caleb because that's what she knew she had to do.

"Can you pull it out?" Janiss whispered as loud as she could.

Caleb seemed to understand. He took hold of the stake with one hand, then tugged. Janiss endured the pain on the promise that, if he could get it out, it would finally stop.

"Try again. Both hands. Whatever it takes."

Using both hands and putting his foot on the door beside her, Caleb yanked harder, and the stake pulled free. The moment it was out, Janiss felt the wound close but not heal. The lack of constant pain was the most wonderful thing she had ever felt.

"He did it?" Ian called ahead, stepping out of the back door.

Not fully recovered, Janiss managed to stand herself up and stepped between Ian and Caleb. "Leave him alone."

She glanced over her shoulder to see if Caleb was smart enough to run, but he just stood there. Why wouldn't he run?

Dammit...

She looked back at Ian, mustering her courage and

using as threatening a tone as she could. "He's *mine*."

"Yours?" Ian asked with suspicious. "You're calling dibs?"

It sounded even more foolish when she heard herself actually say it out loud, but it didn't matter. "I'm not going to let you kill him."

"All right. I won't kill him."

Janiss waited for something more. "You won't?"

Ian shrugged. "What else did you want? You claimed him, so he's your responsibility. He also has a pretty good idea of what you are. Think he'll go to the cops?"

Janiss had rarely heard Caleb speak at all. Could he explain it or even try? Other than her, Ian hadn't actually killed anyone else that she knew of, or at least she hadn't seen it; but where did the blood keep coming from?

Taking her new charge by the shoulder, Janiss gave Ian a warning glance as she walked Caleb past him and back into the kitchen through the back door. She opened the refrigerator to grab a few more of the apples inside but only found two remaining; there had been twelve originally. Other food was missing as well. Daniel hadn't been there long enough to have eaten all of that, so where did it go?

Janiss took the apples outside and gave them to Caleb, then ordered him away. As he left, Janiss walked back out to the garage where Ian stood waiting for her, having never moved.

"Yes?" he said with a sarcastic tone.

"Where is the blood coming from?"

"Do you really want to know?"

"Yes. I do." Janiss didn't flinch. She was tired of his games and intended to call him on every bluff.

Ian seemed impressed. "Come with me."

Janiss followed Ian down the side of the house, across the road to the other side of the property, and down to the utility building. She glanced up the road to see Caleb disappearing in the distance just at the edge of the light. Ian opened the door to the loft and stepped inside with Janiss close behind.

Up the stairs and into the main room, Ian flipped on the light. Two scraggly-looking hunters sat motionless across from one another, blinking occasionally but otherwise non-responsive.

"May I present," Ian said with a grand gesture, "the Connelly blood bank."

"You've been feeding off them?"

"*We've* been feeding off them," he corrected. "And feeding them in return. After a few days, I'll send them on their way with a pocket full of cash that they'll blow on beer."

Janiss guessed that they must have been the poachers that the officer was looking for that morning. "Is this what you do all the time?"

"No," Ian admitted. "One's usually enough for me. *We* don't need much if we stay hydrated. For both of us, we needed more."

"How do you send them on their way so they don't tell anyone?"

"They're in thrall. See how they looked glazed over,

like they've had too much to drink? The door's open but the lights aren't on upstairs. Their short term memory isn't recording anything." To emphasize his point, he made a knocking motion in the air accompanied by the appropriate noise.

Janiss was beginning to understand. "This is what you did to me. This is why I can't remember what happened."

"I told you I didn't rape you."

As if that made it better somehow.

"What you *did* do was as bad or worse!" she shouted. "Look what you're doing to them!"

He laughed. "You mean feeding them to you?"

"Send them away. *Now.*"

Chapter 27

Janiss let the hot water pour over her head. She hadn't had a shower in days and hated the way her hair felt. Sleeping in a shallow grave wasn't conducive to a beauty regimen. She even considered a schedule of washing her hair and putting it up after a productive evening of killing people so she would only have to take a shower after the sun went down.

The scent of her body wash was a new experience. She could smell every ingredient, especially the chemical ones. Her shampoo and conditioner were the same way, perfumed to make them smell like something they weren't. It would be interesting to go shopping again with that little talent.

While the hole through her chest had closed, it hadn't healed. Ian suggested it wouldn't until she went to ground, so if she went out in public, anything low cut or backless would draw the wrong kind of attention.

Janiss didn't want to wait too long for her hair to dry, so she dared to use the dreaded hair dryer on the "air" setting and was surprised how well it turned out. Her complexion was changing, too. She didn't have the usual blemishes she needed to conceal and it only took a light base and eyeliner to finish her face. That countess she read about in history class might have been onto something with those baths, virgin blood or not.

When Janiss emerged from her bedroom at last, Ian was slumped in the easy chair flipping through satellite channels.

"Got a hot date?" he asked.

"Are they gone?"

"With pockets overflowing. What do you suggest we do to feed ourselves now, genius?"

Janiss smirked. "Steal a bloodmobile?"

"Sort of the opposite of drive-thru. Creative. Where are you going?"

"Why do I have to be going anywhere to look nice?"

"Who said you looked nice?" Ian looked down at her purse. "You have your sexy boots on and your purse shouldered. I presume you're going out to eat?"

"I'm going to see Louisa. Want to come along?"

Ian frowned. "Not just yet."

"Well, you can't stay here much longer. Checkout for the Hotel Connelly is Sunday, so you have until then to decide where and when you're going to destroy one another."

"Have a good time, then. Don't do anything I wouldn't do."

Janiss walked out, got into her car and drove off. She smiled as she thought about leaving him there like that. It didn't really matter if she was there or not. Ian did as he pleased and she was done with playing the tortured babysitter.

Literally.

Once she reached the main road, she took her

phone out of her purse and set it in the center console. Halfway to the bridge out to Butcher's Run, she got a signal and a voicemail alert. Finding the same spot as before, she pulled over and checked the message. Her father's voice was unsettling but filled her with longing.

"Hey, Sweetie. Did Daniel make it out okay? Didn't get an answer on the house phone. Hope you're having a good break. We love you."

Her finger hovered over the delete button on the touch screen for a moment, then slid over and tapped the callback instead. The phone began to ring. Janiss placed it close to her ear and waited for an answer.

"Hmm? Hello?"

Janiss felt like she was ten again, and it was a welcome feeling. "Hi, Daddy."

"Sweetie? It's...it's after midnight. Is everything okay?"

"Sure," she lied. "I just really needed to hear your voice."

"Starting to regret skipping the family Thanksgiving to play house at your Gramma's, huh?"

There it was, the understatement of her life.

"It's not too late," he added. "You could come up tomorrow, or make it a day trip on Thanksgiving. Daniel's parents might like to see him, too."

Janiss pulled the phone away from her cheek and pressed the mute button. Why did he have to mention Daniel like that? She closed her eyes, trying hard not to cry but also knowing she only had a few moments to recover before her father would start to worry.

"Sweetie? You still there?"

Maybe she could play cute and dumb while changing the subject. Janiss unmuted the phone and asked, "Play house?"

"Well, you're not a kid anymore and we know you like Daniel. He's a good guy. Just as long as you clean up after yourselves. Other people sleep in those beds, you know."

"Daddy!" She couldn't believe what her father was insinuating.

Of course, he wasn't wrong; but sounding incensed was better than sounding on the verge of tears. Then, again, her father's long-standing insistence on having a man around anywhere she might be alone had also never set well with her.

"Sorry, Sweetie," her father said with a chuckle.

Janiss kept her angry tone. "I still don't know why you won't trust me to take care of myself."

"Well, your mother and I don't want you to wind up like Sis Linn."

That was an odd reference. "The Ghost of Clark Hall? C'mon, Daddy. Halloween was over a few weeks ago."

Her father had graduated from Glenville State College, one of the many reasons she had applied there to study teaching. He was also big into ghost stories, which was another reason he liked Daniel.

Taking on the tone of a horror movie host, he continued. "Every Halloween, stories of the ghost of Sis Linn haunting the buildings on campus run rampant.

Everyone tries to be the first one to tell the story to all the underclassmen, but it was also a terrible tragedy. The poor woman was a teacher for most of her life, married in her fifties, was abandoned by her husband after a few months, and they found her murdered a few years later."

She already knew the story. "Up late watching movies again, huh?"

"You're not the only one on vacation. Have you ever seen her grave? It's in the cemetery just down the hill from the old iron fence."

"Daniel dragged me back there one time. There are graves everywhere..."

"You have to look for her full name: Sarah Louisa Linn."

Louisa?

No. That couldn't have been a coincidence.

"Sarah *Louisa* Linn?" Janiss asked. "You're sure?"

"Sure I'm sure. Have I *finally* piqued your interest in the supernatural, instead of all those romance novels you used to read?"

"Mystery novels, Daddy." Janiss tried not to laugh. "I'll let you go back to sleep now. Give Mom a kiss for me."

"Okay. Nudge Daniel and tell him we'll talk later."

Janiss made an obstinate growl, knowing her father would get it.

"I love you, Sweetie."

"Love you, too." It felt bizarre saying that after all that had happened in the last few days. The phone suddenly felt very heavy in her hand. "Nite-nite, Daddy."

"Nite-nite to you, too."

The call clicked off. She wondered for a moment if she would ever see him again.

Chapter 28

Janiss drove right past the split-lane turn to the Butcher's Run bridge and headed straight on into town. Turning onto Route 33, she drove up the hill through the back entrance onto the Glenville State College campus.

It was impossible for anyone to describe the school without using the word "hills." The campus buildings were nestled close together with one overlooking another. Small cars with no power spent more time sliding down hills than driving over them when it rained – and snow only made it more treacherous. Fortunately, Janiss was experienced with steep inclines from back in her hometown of St. Clairsville, Ohio. Daniel had taught her how to drive there and she had little trouble navigating the roadway.

Security lights illuminated the gymnasium and the parking lot below. There was only one other vehicle in the lot, one covered with two days of snow. She parked her car, pocketed the flashlight she kept in the center console and locked the vehicle remotely before walking across the campus.

Next to the gym was Clark Hall, one of the oldest buildings at the school and reputed to be haunted. It always looked very presidential to her, too much like a residence to be mistaken for a mere courthouse or other government building. Four slender white columns framed the door of the two-story red brick and white wood-trimmed building.

The steps continued down the hillside to Louis Bennet Hall and the cemetery came right up to the back windows of the first floor of the former dormitory. From the next landing down, Janiss walked across the side yard into the cemetery itself.

The Forestry Department had made the cemetery their pet project, including signs, benches and clearing out the undergrowth. The steep incline up and around the path through the headstones was a chore on days when snow wasn't on the ground, but Janiss still found it remarkably easy to walk through, even if it meant her boots would pay the price walking in the snow.

As she started making her way down toward the center of the cemetery, she noticed the snow was gone. Looking ahead, she saw an enclosed group of graves squared in with an iron fence. The patches of grass inside were unusually green in the sunlight.

Sunlight? How could the sun be up?

Janiss stopped and looked around. It was a spring day on the college campus. She could see other students across the way walking up toward Clark Hall. There was a light breeze blowing down from the top of the hill.

"It's just down here," Daniel said as he pushed past her.

It wasn't just a ghost; it was an entire hallucination.

Janiss could only assume that she was literally daydreaming. The detail was incredible; but what was funny was that it all seemed vividly familiar. It was their first year at the school together, a memory she could barely recall.

"Inside the fence?" she heard herself say – only she hadn't said it. Not then, anyway.

"Nope." He almost skipped down around the fence to the second grave past it and rapped his knuckles on it. "Here she is."

Janiss read the writing on the marker. "Sarah Louisa Linn. 1853 to 1919. I thought her name was 'Sis'."

She hadn't remembered that they found the grave, not until right then. It felt like the first time she had seen it, but she knew it wasn't. Even Daniel was vivid, from the stubble he called a mustache to the mud on the side of his black tennis shoes. Every detail was there for the taking.

Daniel shrugged. "It was probably a nickname or something that got started as a rumor." He pointed up to Clark Hall. "See those windows? Her ghost has been seen there and inside the building. Some say she even walks around right here on certain nights when the moon is right."

Janiss made a sound that she thought was appropriately spooky and ghost-like, trying to get into the spirit of the outing. "So why does she haunt Clark Hall and the old cemetery, Dungeon Master?"

"They say," he continued with mock seriousness, "that she still looks for her murderer."

Janiss grinned for a moment, then became more serious. "They don't know who killed her or why?"

"Nope. They say she had money, maybe making

homemade wine with the girls at her boarding house next to where Clark Hall stands now. Sis Linn's body was found beaten beyond recognition, but nothing was stolen. The mystery remains unsolved to this day and that's why her spirit can never rest."

"That's terrible." She looked around the graveyard, remembering that she felt a chill. "This is why you brought me here?"

Daniel smiled that all-is-forgiven smile of his. "It's history. It happened right here. You don't find that even a little interesting?"

"No!" Janiss looked disgusted. "A poor woman was brutalized and her killer got away with it. It's a horrible story; thanks for sharing. Can we go now?"

"You're not scared, are you?" Daniel leaned over the grave with wide eyes, pretending that he was floating toward her like a disembodied spirit.

"Stop it!" she said with a grin, leaning closer to let him kiss her. He was cute when he tried to look scary, like a growling puppy.

For a moment, everything was as it had been. Daniel was being silly, cheering her up and they were doing something together. College life was all about no-money fun; but Janiss always suspected Daniel pushed his horror fetish on her to make her uneasy and want to feel closer to him for reassurance. It wasn't the worst ploy and it was so very Daniel.

In spite of her good feeling, Janiss began to feel unsettled and aggressive. She could smell blood, warm blood, and it was very close.

"Kind of late for Halloween, isn't it?"

It wasn't Daniel's voice. Daniel had vanished.

Who said that?

Janiss found herself standing in the graveyard next the headstone in her vision, Louisa's grave. It was nighttime again and snow was on the ground everywhere.

Just down the hill, a young man was leaning against a tombstone. He looked familiar, maybe an RA at Goodwin Hall. It bothered her that she had been so completely preoccupied with her high-definition trip down memory lane that she had completely missed that he was there. Was that normal? She was less than a few feet away from an easy meal with no one around to stop her from indulging in it...except herself.

She imagined Ian announcing a vampire pop quiz.

There was a flash of flame as the guy lit a cigarette. "Sorry. Hope I didn't scare you."

"Not at all," she replied with a smile.

What was that? Her tone sounded seductive. Why would she try to seduce him?

"I'm Jimmy. You're Janiss, right?" Jimmy stood up and stepped closer.

Janiss wished he hadn't done that.

"Wow," he said. "Most girls around here don't look at me like that."

She was trying very hard to see him as anything other than a full decanter. "Why would you think that? You're handsome enough."

Stop it, she told herself. It was just too easy.

"So, where's Daniel?" he asked. "You two still

dating?"

She thought of Daniel. In the cellar. Mangled. She really didn't want Jimmy to end up like that.

"Are you all right?" Jimmy asked. "You looked kind of spooked all of a sudden."

Janiss smiled for reassurance. "I'm fine. I was doing a little research for a paper I'm writing about Sis Linn."

"Why?" he snickered. "It's all online."

Jimmy the Ever-Helpful and Foolishly-Close-To-Having-His-Throat-Ripped-Out Co-Ed took out a touch-screen phone and tapped up a browser. He did a quick search for Sis Linn at GSC and selected what she guessed was a familiar website to him.

"Here," he said, handing his phone to her.

Janiss held her breath and accepted it. She skimmed the article.

"'Sarah Louisa Linn was born in Fairmont, West Virginia, in 1853, daughter of Robert Linn and Sophronia (Newcomb) Linn.'"

Her mother's maiden name. She'd taken it.

"Jimmy, do you know if Sis Linn's parents are buried out here?"

"Yeah. Right there where I was smoking."

Janiss shined her light further down the hill. An older and more ornate headstone shaped like a tiny arch displayed the names of Louisa's parents. Janiss looked around at where the Admin building, Louis Bennet Hall and Clark Hall were all situated around the cemetery.

"She visits her parents' grave," Janiss realized.

Jimmy took another drag on his cigarette. "Hmm.

That's a pretty good theory. Maybe you should write about that."

Janiss looked back at Jimmy's phone.

"In June of 1905, Sarah Linn married I.L. Chrisman."

Ian.

"Jimmy, I could kiss you."

"Really?"

Janiss was beginning to understand what Ian had meant about distraction. If she wasn't thinking about her thirst or easy prey, she could distract herself thinking about something else. Jimmy was perfectly safe as long as she didn't linger much longer or he didn't do anything stupid.

Still, what she had seen Ian do to the cop out at the church and the hunters intrigued her. Was it something she had to learn, or was it innate? She remembered Louisa telling her that her voice had a different quality to it.

Taking advantage of Jimmy's attention, Janiss met his eyes and made sure he was looking back. "I *could* kiss you," she said, trying to compel him to obey by sheer will, "but smoking's nasty. You should quit."

Janiss put his phone into his hand and left him standing there looking dumbfounded. After she put a little distance between them, she turned to see him drop his cigarette to the ground and step it out.

Chapter 29

It was three in the morning.

Janiss pushed the button on the call box. She wondered if she should have called ahead, but she was almost there already before she thought of it.

"Welcome to Cedarcrest," answered a different voice than she was used to. "Is this a delivery or an emergency?"

Janiss leaned out and looked up at the nearest thing she thought was a camera. "Tell Timothy that Janiss Connelly is here."

The box clicked off. After a few moments, a buzzer sounded and the gates opened.

As she was parking her car, she noticed the lobby interior lights change from white to red. People inside were moving quickly and disappeared into various hallways and elevators. By the time she crossed the goggle-eyed, fang-faced seal to the front doors, the lobby was empty.

She wondered if she was really that dangerous.

Behind the main desk, the center elevator opened by itself. To her surprise, two men she had never seen before stood inside looking like bouncers from a nightclub, both with upper arms almost as big around as their thighs. One had a dark goatee while the other had a little blonde patch on his chin. They were easily a head taller than Janiss and probably three times her weight. Each had a belt like a policeman equipped with a two-foot long baton.

Were they waiting for her?

Whatever.

Janiss walked around the desk and stepped into the elevator, wondering how she would react. They were definitely on the menu, judging by her throat going dry and the way her muscles tensed. It seemed stupid to her that Louisa would clear her staff out of the lobby and send down two cows for her.

"What are you two supposed to be? Hors d'oeuvres?"

Both men tensed at the remark but probably thought she couldn't tell.

She smirked. It didn't suck being feared a little.

The elevator door opened on the upper floor into the hallway ending at Louisa's office. She saw both Louisa and Timothy stepping out as if to meet her. Janiss walked briskly toward them. When she was almost halfway, she saw Louisa nod in her direction but not at her.

The footfalls of the two bouncers sounded as they ran up behind her.

Flashing Louisa a look of betrayal, Janiss turned in time to see the goatee bouncer leaping for her midsection. To her surprise, she sidestepped the lunge easily; but the move lined her up with the patch bouncer, allowing him to shove her to the ground. He straddled her, pinning her hips with his weight and pressing her wrists down with his massive arms.

Janiss didn't know how to fight, but her father had paid for her to take a few self-defense courses – just enough for his little girl to get away should the need arise. The dominant hold of the huge man over a tiny woman was classic, but fortunately it was one of the escapes she knew.

The only way an attacker could apply force was in one direction at a time. After pulling her arms down to her sides, she dipped the bouncer toward her face and bucked her hips. Done quickly and correctly, the maneuver should have been enough to throw him over her head so she could roll away.

The bouncer went flying instead, almost to Louisa's feet.

By that time, the goatee bouncer was back up and coming at Janiss again, but this time with a stake in his hand. She didn't even see where it had come from.

Remembering the constant torture of being impaled, the sight of the stake triggered an immediate transformation. With eyes blackened and fangs bared, she slashed her talons at the man's arm holding the stake. Two of her fingers found their mark. The man shrieked and dropped the stake, grasping his arm as the blood started to flow.

"Enough!" Louisa commanded.

Janiss turned away from the wounded bouncer, focusing instead on the man she had bucked onto the floor. The less blood she saw, the better – and being pissed at Louisa for the ambush made it easier to focus.

She walked to the downed bouncer and offered him a hand getting to his feet, just to show Louisa up.

"Janiss," she offered in friendship.

"Cole," he said, and accepted her hand. He looked defeated but impressed.

Louisa, on the other hand, sounded as cold as ever. "Take Travis down to the infirmary and get him cleaned up before he bleeds all over my carpet."

Cole caught up with his wounded friend at the elevator. Janiss could hear them whispering to one another as the doors closed.

"I like her," Cole said.

"You're not the one bleeding," Travis countered.

Janiss collected the stake Travis had dropped. As she took it back to Louisa, she looked at her fingertips as tiny droplets of blood disappeared into her skin.

"I'm keeping this," she told Louisa as she pushed past her into the office. "It will go nicely next to the one your ex-husband stabbed me with earlier this evening."

Louisa followed Janiss in and closed the door with Timothy still outside. "Something on your mind, child?" Her tone was irritable, like she was itching for a fight.

Good.

"For one thing," Janiss replied while waving the stake for emphasis, "I'm tired of you calling me that."

"Perhaps you should stop acting like one."

"And what's with the goons in the elevator?"

"They work part time for me when not working at the prison. That, as you put it, was practice. For them, by the way, not you. It's clear they need a lot more after seeing that pathetic display."

Louisa flipped open one of her laptops and pressed a few keys, but Janiss wasn't going to be ignored.

"Am I interrupting your status update?"

Louisa continued to stare intently at her screen.

"Aren't you at least going to ask me about how I know about your marriage to Ian....*Sarah*?"

Louisa glanced up, the pale light from the screen illuminating the underside of her face, making it look very sinister. "What do you think you know...*Janiss*?"

Janiss ignored the return volley. "I get that Ian came back after a few years and turned you or whatever it is you call it..."

"No!" Louisa slammed the laptop closed; it sounded as though the screen might have shattered. "He did *not* come back later to make me. He courted and married me – and on our wedding night, he took me to bed and turned me!" she seethed. "Then he dropped me into the ground. I awoke the next evening buried alive and my world destroyed. Sound familiar?"

That wasn't what I was I expecting, thought Janiss. She asked in a softer tone, "He killed you on your wedding night?" If Louisa was married in 1905, why did her tombstone read 1919?

"He wanted me to go with him," Louisa explained, "two immortals having their way with the world. All I wanted was someone to love me for the rest of my life, and I was already in my fifties! When I begged him to fix it, to destroy me if there was no other way, he abandoned me. I didn't know what to do or how to survive.

Pretending to still be alive was the only thing I had left."

Janiss felt ashamed. "I'm so sorry that happened to you."

"And to *you*. Don't you understand? It's not just us. How many others has he done this to? How many more lives has he continued to destroy?"

"Then what's all this?" Janiss indicated everything around her and where she was standing. "Why build this if all you want to do is kill him or die trying?"

"An immortal has nothing if not time," Louisa answered. "There's also no such thing as a poor old vampire. It's easy for us to amass wealth and I felt compelled to do something with it. Those plans will continue long after I'm gone and I would very much like them to include you."

"Me? I can't run this place."

"Timothy knows what to do. There's a board. Directors. Doctors. People you haven't met. We're doing something wonderful here, taking death and turning it into life. The source is potent but limited. Do you understand?"

Janiss shook her head.

"It's us. Our blood has regenerative and anti-catalytic properties, but the potency is very restricted. Once the rest of this business is behind us, you'll be the source, Janiss. You have a good heart. You seem to have retained it."

While the science escaped her, Janiss was catching on. "You were going to turn me yourself, weren't you?"

Finding out how and when Louisa was turned had

tempered Janiss's demeanor; but the realization that Louisa had almost the same thing in mind for her as what Ian did wasn't winning her any points. Louisa was starting to sound as manipulative as her ex.

Composing herself, Louisa stepped around the table as if she were floating, gliding with each step as she moved toward her. "That's how I used to do it, you know."

"Do what? Stalk your next meal?"

"Haunt the Old Glenville Cemetery. I stopped doing it years ago, but it's a simple step. I'd appear every few years, sometimes in the graveyard or inside one the buildings. Once in a while, a student would catch me and we would talk. Cemeteries aren't important to the dead, Janiss. I encouraged the Forestry Department to clean up the area some years ago. Places like that are full of memories."

Janiss realized something. "Who's buried in your grave if you were already dead?"

"Eleanor," Louisa answered in a dismissive tone. "I never knew her last name."

That obviously meant more to Louisa than she let on. Janiss was irritated that her original question was being ignored, but she wanted all the information she could get and chose not to interrupt.

"Once I started to figure out how to survive, I opened a boarding house for young women who wanted to be teachers. A select few I trusted well enough to learn and keep my secret. Some of the others accused me of being militant with the house rules, likening me to a

Catholic nun and calling me Sister Linn when they thought I couldn't hear them."

Janiss could well imagine them calling Louisa militant, but the person actually in Louisa's grave seemed important. "Was Eleanor one of the girls at the house?"

Louisa looked hurt when Janiss repeated the name again. "No, she was my friend. She had run away from a bad marriage and we connected over that."

Feeling like she was intruding on something painful, Janiss stopped pressing her. "So what made you decide to pursue Ian after starting the boarding house?"

"It haunted me knowing he was still out there and might be harming others. I started to see a return on my investments. He wasn't trying to stay hidden, at least not from someone who knew what to look for. I exposed him by seeding a few anonymous tips to the police, and he didn't take kindly to it. He came back to Glenville to confront me, but..."

She trailed off and grew very quiet.

"Louisa?" Janiss looked thoughtfully at her.

"Eleanor was deathly afraid of her husband, of him finding her. She came to the boarding house and begged me to hide her and I did. No one in the house knew she was staying in my rooms; but when Ian came for me, he found her hiding there."

Janiss recalled the end of article. "Sarah" was reportedly found beaten beyond recognition – but it hadn't been Louisa.

"Many people had already mistaken her for me when they found her, " Louisa continued. "I hadn't aged for some time, so it was my chance to disappear and become someone else."

Timothy came into the room. He was holding another tall black coffee cup.

"Why did Ian attack Eleanor so brutally?" The moment Janiss spoke her mind, she realized she hadn't meant to sound so cold.

Louisa's expression soured into a frightening mask of hatred, the corners of her eyes wet with blood. "Feel free to ask him when you see him next."

"You should ask him yourself."

"Louisa never leaves the facility," Timothy commented with a smirk.

He handed the coffee cup to Janiss. She held it for a few moments before drinking it properly and not like she was dying of thirst.

"You're getting stronger very quickly," Louisa observed, leaving the other conversation behind. "I think I chose well."

Janiss took another drink. "You didn't answer my original question," she said with a darker tone. "You intended to turn me yourself, didn't you?"

Timothy looked expectantly at Louisa. She didn't react to it.

"Yes...dear," Louisa admitted. "I thought we had more time. It was completely by chance that Ian arrived when he did, that he made you instead of killing you outright."

"Were you even going to give me a choice?" Janiss's voice grated in her ears. She didn't like sounding so hateful, but she had a right to.

Louisa drew closer, folding her hands in front of her. "I know I can come off as cold, but I wouldn't have asked you to do this if I didn't think you could handle it. Did I not give you the choice to stay here under my protection rather than confront Ian?"

"You did." Janiss drained the cup. "Knowing what he is, what he's like, why would you insist on sending me back to him?"

"You have power. He forced it onto you. He didn't ask and he didn't give; he chose *for* you. If you had refused my offer, that would have been the end of it. The least he could do is show you what can be done with it, but he can't hurt you anymore unless you let him."

"He's hurt me plenty." Janiss didn't enjoy it, but she understood the idea. "You wanted me to see him for what he really is."

"And to stand up for yourself. Don't let this ruin you; face your demon. You're also a distraction. He will continue doing this to others in the future unless I deal with him. I need you to maneuver him here – and I really want him to think it's his idea."

Chapter 30

Janiss came through the kitchen and into the living room. Ian looked like he hadn't moved since she left for town, still in the easy chair watching something on the television with people screaming and bleeding. Without a word, she walked past him into her bedroom and dropped off her purse and coat.

"So, professor," Janiss finally acknowledged him. "What's the lesson plan for tomorrow night?"

Ian muted the program and sat up. "How's Louisa?"

"*Sarah* is just fine. She asked about you."

Ian seemed either interested or irritated; it was hard to tell. "Told you the whole sordid story, did she?"

"No. I went up to the college to crawl around the graveyard. I wanted to get a feel for it. You're not that hard to find online in this day and age, Mr. Chrisman."

She saw the look again, the same one she saw when she clawed his face...right before he knocked her across the yard into the garage door. He didn't like anyone getting a leg up on him and now he wasn't sure what Janiss knew or not. She wondered why he would even care; but it was clear that it bothered him.

Either aware that she had noticed – or determined not to be affected by it – Ian changed the subject entirely. "Student's choice. What can I teach you?"

"Combat training."

Ian laughed. "You want to learn how to kill me *from* me, is that it?"

"Or kill Louisa," Janiss countered.

"Hmm. Now you have my attention. Actually, there's really nothing to learn. You're faster and stronger than any human, even one who's combat trained – maybe ten times so. The rules are simple: strike first and hit hard. You never have to defend yourself if your opponent is already defeated."

"What about more than one?" Like a couple of thugs hanging out in an elevator with stakes, she thought to herself.

"Other vampires?" Ian assumed. "Almost an impossibility. We're solitary creatures, all alpha. Packs aren't our thing. We compete too much, take what we want. You could travel hundreds of miles in any direction and not find another one of us; and they don't all know how to make their own kind."

Janiss perked up. "How did you make me?"

"You asked about fighting. One course at a time."

"Fine," she said with a hint of irritation. "Is there a good defense against another vampire?"

"If you've pissed one off you have no chance of defeating? Sure. Run like hell. Otherwise, put them down."

Janiss waited for something more. "That's it?"

"Yep. What? Did you think you'd rise from the grave with the powers of Bruce Lee or something?"

He was such an ass. She hadn't intended to rise

from the grave at all. "All right, so what are we going to do tomorrow night?"

Ian grinned. "I'll think of something, but it's too late to get into anything else tonight before your bedtime. I'd also like to finish watching my movie to see how horribly the rest of the cast dies."

Janiss left Ian to his stupid movie and went into the kitchen.

After spending the evening getting impaled and reliving memories in graveyards, she was on edge and having trouble relaxing. She wanted to do something, anything at all; but she was also well aware that feeling would pass at sunrise. The only thing she would want to do then was crawl into her shallow grave in the cellar and close her eyes.

She didn't need the light on, but she turned it on anyway and looked around the kitchen. There was a round container of a generic hot chocolate mix, the kind you add to hot water or milk, with the stale little marshmallows that turn soft. It reminded her of eating bowls of Count Chocula cereal around Halloween as a kid – did they still make that stuff? Daniel used to keep the boxes around months after the cereal was gone.

Janiss took a mug from a cabinet and filled it with water from the tap, then put it into the microwave to heat it up.

"Can you make me one?" she heard Daniel's voice ask.

It was like some kind of trigger, thinking of Daniel before hearing or seeing him. Why were the visions so vivid?

Janiss turned and looked toward the sound. Daniel was sitting at the kitchen table with puppy dog eyes, his hands folded in front of him while waiting for an answer.

I could, she thought, but you couldn't drink it anyway.

"It wouldn't hurt you to be nice to me," Daniel responded.

She hadn't actually said that, but he commented all the same as if he'd heard it.

Janiss noticed that the kitchen had changed. The tablecloth was different and pans hanging over the window counters were in a different order. It was a memory; it had to be. Why did it feel so interactive? Was Daniel really haunting her, or was she doing it to herself?

"Haven't I always been nice to you?"

Daniel grinned. "You can be distant at times. When we were younger, before you got all girly-girly, you used to drop everything to hang out with me. After your mom convinced you to give up jeans and t-shirts, all that other stuff seemed more important to you."

"It's called 'growing up'."

The microwave beeped. Janiss took the mug out and stirred a couple scoops of the powdery mixture into it. As she sat down at the table across from Daniel, he seemed to be waiting for her. He was interacting and answering her questions. Still, the answers seemed familiar – as if they were made up of different memories. She didn't believe in ghosts; but then, again, she hadn't believed in vampires, either.

"Why are you here?" she asked.

"Do you want me to go?" He started to get up.

"No!" She was surprised how quickly she reacted. "I miss you. Stay and talk to me."

He relaxed and smiled. "There's the Janiss I love, the one who wanted me around."

"I always wanted you around; but you never seemed to grow up and meet me halfway." It was eating away at her, all of the things she always wanted to say to him but had been afraid of saying and hurting his feelings. "How were we supposed to be together if all the responsibility was on me?"

Daniel looked hurt. "Why would you say that to me? You know I hate when we fight."

That was always his excuse. Don't fight and don't scold.

"It's true, Daniel. You're always late and always distracted. When you're with me, really *with* me, it's great. It's all the other times, like when you should have been working on your degree. Did you even have enough credits to graduate? Was I supposed to take care of you just so you could entertain me?"

Daniel scowled. "Whenever you get like this, I don't want to be anywhere near you!"

Janiss smirked. "So I was no fun when it was time for me to work hard and less fun when I demanded it from you. Typical, Daniel."

Saying it made her feel better, but he looked angry. "Fine. Maybe I should leave."

"Good. Go."

"Go where?" Ian asked.

Ian walked into the kitchen. Daniel was gone and the kitchen looked normal again, or at least as it was instead of how she remembered it. She was convinced more than ever that the entire thing was in her head, but she was satisfied with how the conversation went. Her only real regret was that she couldn't have told Daniel in person. It might have even saved his life.

She also wondered how long she had been talking out loud.

"What are you drinking?" Ian asked.

"Hot chocolate," she said. "The instant kind."

"Everything is instant these days. Microwave ovens, information, mail, news, you name it. Nothing happens slowly anymore. It's all so rushed."

"Shouldn't you be standing in the yard telling the kids to get off the lawn?" Janiss took a sip from the cup. "How's it taste?"

"Fake. Everything tastes and smells like chemicals now."

"Yeah. It's the processing. Your palette is as refined as all of your other senses. You can clearly hear whispers, feel a fingerprint on a pane of glass. You can perceive the imperfections in things you used to think were perfect."

Janiss sighed. "I can see the dust settling back on the counter tops."

"Why do you think vampires stop dusting and cleaning after a few centuries?"

He flashed his clever smile to see if she would return it. She humored him.

"Who were you talking to?" Ian asked.

It embarrassed her a little. She wasn't sure when she started talking out loud instead of in her head. "Daniel."

Ian looked intrigued. "He's haunting you, isn't he? Your kills stay with you, you know. They're part of you."

Brimming with confidence, she called him on his attempted deception. "I don't think there are such things as ghosts, Ian, and it wasn't him. I know it wasn't, but why did it seem so vivid?"

Ian looked flustered having been caught in a lie. It was nice to see him having a human moment. "You're tripping."

"And you're full of shit."

"No, I mean what you were doing." Ian laughed. "I call it tripping."

Janiss was at a loss. She looked at her mug. "Like on drugs?"

"Think of it like daydreaming. You don't dream anymore when you're resting, right?"

"Right."

"That's because you're dead. You don't sleep so you can't dream. You have full access to your subconscious and an almost eidetic memory. You can rerun whole scenes in your head and interact with them, even notice details you may have ignored before. It's all in there."

"Neat trick."

"Yeah, but be careful where you perform it. If you get caught up in a daydream, you'll miss what's going on around you." He opened the door to the brightening morning.

"Where are you going?" Janiss asked.

"To where I rest. It wouldn't do for the teacher to get staked before tonight's lesson."

"I can't imagine who would do such a thing. Which isn't fair, by the way, since you know exactly where I sleep." Janiss tried another sip, frowned, and poured the cup out into the sink.

"Hey, at least I made your bed for you. Shouldn't you be in it, young lady?"

"I'm not sleepy yet, evil wicked stepfather." She meant for that to sound clever. He seemed to like it.

"If I could have had a daughter," Ian added, "I wouldn't have hated for her to be like you. I think you're going to turn out all right, Annette."

Ian closed the door behind him and stepped through the snow up the gravel road behind the house. He started at a brisk walk, then took to a run. He was out of sight within a few moments.

"Annette?" Janiss was perplexed as to why he called her by her middle name. "I *have* a father, asshole."

Janiss exhaled and let her anger go. The sun was rising and she wanted the experience of being awake during the day. Could she get used to it? It had been too debilitating on the mountaintop. How did Louisa and Ian do it? Would she have to wait a century? It was frustrating, like having to learn how to walk or read again.

The instant the sun rose, she felt her heart slam to a stop. She had to make a conscious effort to breathe, not that she needed to do so. Her body was weakening as if her strength was bleeding out of her.

She tried to focus, locked the kitchen door and found her way back into the cellar. After peeling off her clothes, she collapsed into her grave – saddened for a moment knowing she wouldn't ever dream again.

Chapter 31

Janiss opened the cellar door.

Ian wasn't at the kitchen table.

She checked the living room and the bedrooms, but he wasn't there either. Out of habit, she put on Daniel's coat to walk outside into the cold night air even though it no longer bothered her in the least. The snow had been melting a little during the day and refreezing at night, making the crust of it brittle; it crunched beneath each footstep as the ice compacted. She circled the property outside, walked behind the garage and checked down by the utility building.

There was no sign of him. Did he oversleep?

Janiss looked in the direction in which Ian had run off. She hadn't been up the old trail to the back of the property in years, not since the last time she and her father had gone for a hike the summer before she started high school. There was a pond up there next to a grove of apple trees and an old hunting cabin that had fallen into ruin decades ago.

It seemed as good a place as any to look.

The trail was simple to find. She found tracks in the snow, too; but it was more than one person. She could tell at a glance it was three men, none of them Ian judging from the boot size.

Weird. When did she become a tracker?

She reached the top of the hill and looked down toward the pond. The pupils of her eyes widened, enhancing the starlight until it was almost daytime to her. There was a light in a clearing next to the ruined cabin coming from inside a tent. Right beside it were two pickup trucks and a quad-runner parked next to a tree clearly marked private property and no trespassing. Her dad would have been furious.

It was only then Janiss realized how famished she was and Ian wasn't there to provide for her. She could go to Louisa again, but she needed to find Ian. He really wouldn't have just left, would he?

She turned her attention back to the poachers. If the idiots couldn't read, they could always pay their campground fee in blood, right? This was her final exam, to see if she could feed herself without taking a life. Ian suggested a little more than a pint would do. Timothy had served her tall coffee mugs, so the amount seemed consistent.

Janiss exhaled and let her muscles swell. With the ground visible and her reflexes primed, she easily slipped down the hillside without a sound and stepped up right next to the tent. Judging by the shadows against the tent, there were three hunters inside and it sounded like they were playing cards. One of them started to get up and reached down to unzip the front.

She started to hide, but decided against it. It was her family's property, after all. If the poachers weren't open to suggestion, she could always tell them to get off her land. If they didn't like that, she could certainly kick their asses, and they could count themselves lucky if she stopped with that.

The zipper opened and a thick young man stepped out. He was big but not huge, wearing camouflaged coveralls pulled down halfway and tied around his waist by the sleeves. The words "show me your tits" were written across his t-shirt.

After he zipped the tent flap back down, he stood up fully and almost walked into Janiss.

"Hey!" he said with a grin.

Janiss was dumbfounded. Was he really that stupid, sizing up a complete stranger in the middle of the woods at night? It wasn't hard for her to justify that he didn't deserve at least a little bit of what was going to happen next.

She gathered her will, fixed her eyes on his, and spoke deliberately.

"Follow me."

The young man's eyes relaxed and he became hers, obeying without question. It worked! It was also nice that learning to use at least one of her abilities didn't require being tortured at the hand of a sadist.

Leading him away from the camp to what she guessed was a safe enough distance, Janiss stopped him and told him to roll up his sleeve. She turned his forearm over to expose the underside.

Her biggest concern was that she wouldn't know when to stop before it was too late, but it also occurred to her that *he* might.

"The moment you feel even a little faint," she

commanded him, "whisper it to me. Do you understand?"

"Yeah."

Janiss lifted the young man's arm to her lips, bared her fangs, and sunk them into his flesh. The warm fluid spilling into her mouth was a forbidden fire, salty and metallic, sweet and intoxicating. She didn't ever want it to stop.

"I'm feeling..." she heard the young man start to say, but he was already falling over. Either he was a serious lightweight or she had lost all track of time. Janiss yanked his arm away and caught him. There was a stupid grin on his face.

"Are you all right?" she whispered. "Can you stand?"

"Yeah," he answered.

She helped him back up and steadied him until he seemed okay, then examined the wound. The flow had stopped well enough that he wouldn't bleed to death. It was neat and clean compared to her last unguided attempt that had ended in murder.

But what to do with him?

"What's your name?" she asked.

"Bobby Truit."

The surname sounded familiar. There were Truits who owned property over the Lewis County line. "Who's in the tent with you?"

"My cousins, Dale and Tommy."

"Are their last names Truit, too?"

"Yep."

Good ol' boys, Janiss thought. Who did they think they were, not only hunting on her family's property but camping out on it? They were exactly the kind of people both her mother and father were afraid would take advantage of her "without a man around," as her father always said.

Okay, enough with the sneaky vampire crap.

She led Bobby back over to the tent, then told him to wake up. She hoped that would work.

Bobby blinked, then looked down at Janiss as if noticing her for the first time. He started to say "hey" again until he noticed the sour expression on her face. His hand drifted to his arm as he probably noticed the pain of her bite.

"What are you doing on my family's property?" Janiss said it loud enough that the men inside the tent could hear her clearly.

The other two ruffians spilled out of the tent, one with his hand on his sidearm. Janiss played it up as if she already knew who they were.

"Dale and Tommy Truit! You know what my daddy would do to you if he caught you three on our land?" She shot a stern glance at the one with the holster. "Get your hand off that gun."

Both men initially had the same look on their faces as Bobby until she said their names. They looked at one another as if trying to figure out how she knew them, but they already looked guilty as sin.

"Sorry, ma'am," one of them said. "We didn't think anyone was using this place..."

"You didn't think you'd get *caught*," Janiss replied. "One of our no trespassing signs is stapled to the tree you pitched your tent beside." She pointed it out in case they continued to ignore it. "I assume you can read?"

Again with the looking at each other.

When they didn't answer her, Janiss folded her arms and took a stance. "So start packing it up before I call the sheriff out here to help you!"

With half-annoyed and half-worried expressions, the three of them began to empty the tent and toss things into the backs of their trucks. Janiss watched for a minute, then started to walk away.

"You should also probably get Bobby's arm looked at," she called back over her shoulder. "It looks like something out here bit him."

Janiss walked around the other side of the cabin looking for any place Ian might have crawled into, but he certainly wouldn't have gone to ground so close to the Truits. It occurred to her that Ian might have wanted her to see him leaving in that direction. He might have lead her there on purpose, knowing that the hunters were camped out and she needed to feed.

She had to tell Louisa that Ian was missing.

Chapter 32

Back at the house, Janiss gave all the rooms one last look through, including the upstairs room that was usually locked up. Ian wasn't there. If it was true that he left, he might be heading out to Louisa. Wasn't that why he had come back to Glenville in the first place?

She checked the house phone in the hallway. It was working; Ian might have had nothing to do with that at all. After pulling up a chair, she looked up Timothy's number from her mobile phone and tapped it into the house phone.

"Hello, Ms. Connelly," Timothy said as he answered. It wasn't a warm tone, but it didn't sound as unfeeling as it usually did. Also, Janiss had just called from a different phone.

"How did you know it was me?"

"It's one of the numbers you filled out on your paperwork for Louisa."

It made sense.

Timothy sighed. "Was there something in particular that you needed?"

"I think I've lost Ian."

"One moment." The phone clicked, then the sound changed. He probably put it on speaker.

"How are you doing this evening, Janiss?" Louisa asked as she came on. Her voice sounded less bitter than usual, too.

"Ian wasn't here this evening. We talked last night..."

"What about?" She sounded concerned.

"I called him by his full name. He was evasive, then later said something about not hating me if I could have been his daughter."

"Anything else?"

"That he thought I'd be okay. I guess he meant as a vampire."

Louisa was quiet, then said, "He might have left, or he might want you to think so."

"I looked around." Janiss considered how much to tell Louisa. "I even managed to find a meal and not kill anyone."

"Well done. We'll wait and watch for him here. I don't believe he came all this way to play father figure and scamper off."

"What should I do?"

"Wait there tonight. If he doesn't come back and we don't hear anything, come to out to Cedarcrest tomorrow night."

"Happy Thanksgiving," Janiss whispered to herself, not intending for anyone else to hear it.

"You, too, Janiss." The tone was sorrowful; Louisa understood missing family.

Janiss hung up the phone.

She had no idea how long she would have to wait.

Chapter 33

Midnight.

No sign of Ian.

One o' clock and still nothing.

Two o' clock, then almost three.

It was Thanksgiving morning, and Janiss hadn't moved for hours. She looked into the empty kitchen and remembered seeing her mother and Gramma up early, getting the turkey into the oven for an afternoon dinner. Mashed potatoes that weren't from a mix, pumpkin pie made from an actual pumpkin and bread stuffing cooked inside the bird.

The house had been filled with the smells of food and the voices of family and friends. She had loved being surrounded by parents, grandparents, her mother's sister and her cousins – and even Daniel and his parents on two occasions. Just happy people visiting and talking. It didn't matter if it was the morning parades, the afternoon football games, or card games in the kitchen at night.

It was enough to make her want to burn everything to the ground so she wouldn't have to see it empty.

"I've got to get out of here," she said to no one.

Janiss looked back up at the wall through the pictures again. There *was* someone she could spend Thanksgiving morning with who would be safe for her to do so, and she missed them as much as anyone.

She put on Daniel's pea coat, grabbed her keys and walked out the door to her car.

Chapter 34

Ian listened intently until he could no longer hear the sound of Janiss's departing vehicle. He had picked a good spot across the road from which to watch the house and saw her make a phone call. Knowing how bad his own cell reception was out in the sticks, it was a short list of who she might be calling so late in the evening.

He strolled down the hillside out of the pines and crossed the creek at a narrow point. Past the utility building and across the road, Ian wasn't surprised to find the side door unlocked and let himself in.

Seating himself in the same chair where Janiss had been sitting, he lifted the old push-button telephone receiver and pressed the redial button. He smiled when he heard a series of clicks instead of touch-tones, the sound of a bygone era before computers could fit in someone's pocket.

"Did you have some additional information, Ms. Connelly?" the droll voice on the other end answered.

Ian leaned back and made himself comfortable. "I'd like to speak to the vampire of the house, please."

There was a moment's hesitation. "Mr. Chrisman, I presume?"

"You can presume whatever you like, Chuckles. Put my ex-wife on the horn."

"She's indisposed..."

"I said put Sarah on the phone, you little fuck!" Ian shouted into the receiver, the plastic cracking under his grip. "Do it or I'll stake her little protégé, cut her up with a butter knife and feed her to you a pound of flesh at a time!"

There was another pause.

"I think you're bluffing," Timothy replied in a cool tone. "Sarah doesn't wish to speak with you at this moment."

Ian thought about it, composed himself, then grinned. "Does Janiss know you Lo-Jacked her car?"

Timothy ignored the question. "Did you care to leave a message?"

"Absolutely, since I'm sure you've got me on speakerphone and she's listening right now. I'm flattered you wanted me to come back to our old alma mater for a tryst, Sarah; but making Janiss reminded me of just how important it is for the older generation to connect with today's disillusioned youth. Therefore, I've decided to rescind my acceptance of your obvious invitation to throw down and will instead disappear into the wind forever. I hope you and Janiss and whoever you're eating over there in that ivory tower of yours have a long, lonely, boring fucking eternity."

Ian hung the phone back on its hook and laughed. He half expected it to ring back, but he wasn't surprised when it didn't.

He got up to leave, but the pictures on the wall in the hallway distracted him. Most were very recent; but some were old, very old, from times he remembered. He had looked at them all before, especially the ones of Janiss as a child with her grandparents. There was a lot of love there, the kind of influence that shapes someone for the rest of their life.

Good for her.

On any other occasion, he would have had someone torch the farmhouse. He liked watching things burn. Fire was a force of nature that consumed everything in its path, something he admired. The farmhouse belonged to Janiss, even if it was her father's name on the paperwork. Who was he to destroy her childhood home? That right belonged to her and no one else.

He had lit a flame inside Janiss, whether she realized it or not. He had fanned it and watched it grow. After her insistence that he let the hunters go, it had been a simple thing to compel the Truits to relocate their hunting camp and wait around to be slaughtered. Janiss had remembered the way Ian had left, following his breadcrumbs to a free meal. She could have just as easily killed them, but she managed to satiate herself without the need to dispose of any remains.

Ian almost felt bad for her. He hadn't been so strong when he rose for the first time. There were terrible things he had done before his death, although none of them compared to what he did after. Janiss was holding onto something. He wasn't sure whether it was the house, her family, or her dead boyfriend; but it was keeping her sane through her transformation into a predator. When she finally gave in and realized how little it all really meant to an immortal, it would destroy her.

After taking a final stroll around the old farmhouse, he closed the back door behind him and hiked over the hill in the direction of the hidden Escalade. It wasn't bravado; seeing Janiss blossoming into a killer made him wonder why he had waited so many years to sire another vampire. Janiss might have been an exception; but he was growing curious as to what could be done with someone with the predisposition to be a killer rather than be made into one.

First things first, however. He didn't want to spend the holiday looking like Farmer Connelly, and shopping at the local Wally World was out of the question. It was only an hour up I-79 to Meadowbrook Mall in Bridgeport.

Shouldn't everyone dress nice for the holiday?

Chapter 35

Janiss parked her car in front of the Locust Knob Church of Christ. It was always sad to see the little church closed up and unused, but there just weren't enough people around to use it anymore.

She walked around the side of the building into the cemetery and up one of the four rows of headstones. She always knew right were to look; she'd attended their funerals, after all.

The wide, arched headstone announced the occupants: Ellis and Jenetta Sumpter. They were just Gramma and Grampa to her; and it was years before she had even bothered to learn their real names. As they grew older and started slowing down, even turning the reigns of the family Thanksgiving dinner over to her parents, they were an integral part of the holiday. It was never the same after they passed away, and eventually it became too painful to keep the tradition alive in a house of the dead.

Janiss wondered if she should say something to Daniel first, but she wasn't ready for that yet. She could see the mound of dirt where Abe Massey was buried, the most recent occupant of the cemetery. It was also Daniel's hidden grave; and it didn't sit well with her that his parents would never know what happened to their son, a secret meant to protect her own guilt. It was an accident, but that didn't make her feel any less responsible.

Janiss had to laugh at herself. The notion that Louisa haunted the graves of her relatives seemed foolish when she had found out about it; but there she was, standing over her grandparents' headstone doing almost the exact same thing.

"Happy Thanksgiving, Gramma. You too, Grampa."

From the middle of the cemetery at night, the church could have been new or old. The crescent moon and bright starlight made it appear ethereal, a place where spirits could dwell. She didn't enjoy going to church anymore after the funerals, feeling a little mad at God for taking her Gramma and Grampa away.

Was she being punished for that? It seemed a little excessive.

Janiss really did love the little church. It seemed a shame that no one used the building anymore. When was the last time anyone had been inside of it? That, she thought, could be rectified easily enough.

Her eyes were good in starlight, but it would certainly be darker inside the church. She stopped back at her vehicle and grabbed her flashlight from the center console again.

The door on the side of the church wasn't the main door; but the padlock looked old, and she didn't want to damage anything getting in. A moment of concentration and the proper application of vampire strength should just pop the lock, right? She gave the padlock a quick yank but still accidentally ripped the hasp out by the screws, leaving the lock perfectly intact in her hand. Okay, someone else could probably fix that later, but at least the door was ajar.

Janiss pressed the button on her flashlight and pushed the door all the way open. The first thing she saw was the old wooden sign hung on the wall opposite the side door that read "Register of Attendance and Offering." Each row on the sign had a purpose, from the number of bibles brought to the all-time record attendance. The last Sunday offering was ten dollars and thirty-one cents. How long ago had that been?

The moment Janiss crossed the threshold into the church, her senses alerted her to something very wrong. There was an odor, like a rodent that had been trapped inside and died there – but it was different and too much. Why did she also smell apples? She thought of Caleb for a moment but wasn't sure why.

Janiss turned the corner past the alcove just inside the doorway, looking toward the pulpit at the front of the church. Were there figures seated in the pews? One of them was leaning over the podium as if addressing the others.

It made her shudder. She was spooked.

How could anything spook a vampire?

She clicked the light off before she was tempted to shine it in that direction. Being mad at God as a child was one thing – but being a vampire breaking into an abandoned church and finding a congregation waiting for her was a little more than disturbing. Was she imagining them? This was no memory. She couldn't tell what they were and wasn't sure she wouldn't scream if any of them moved.

Allowing her eyes to fully adjust, she could count the shadows: nine, including the one at the front. Glancing back at the register, she realized that the last Sunday attendance was also nine.

Turning her light back on and pointing it at the register again, she looked at the number itself. It shouldn't have been clean, but it was. Someone had cleaned the sign and the lettering before changing the register.

Ten thirty-one? Halloween?

Shit.

No longer fearing the vengeful presence of a divine being, Janiss was very much afraid she just missed the Devil himself.

She aimed her light down the center isle between the pews and up to the podium. The figure there seemed to be leaning on it for support, as if the person couldn't stand up without it. She gasped as the light touched the face.

It was Daniel.

His arms were lashed to the podium with rope. His body was turned in an awkward position to make him appear propped up on his arms. A stick from outside had been jammed up into his lower jaw and wedged against his chest to keep his head looking up. Open between his arms on the podium was a bible, as though he were reading from it.

The flashlight made a popping sound before Janiss

realized she was holding it too tight. She trembled with anger and frustration. It wasn't just that Ian had been lying to her; it was the way he disrespected everything, including the dead.

Before she became a vampire, seeing all of that would have had her in tears; but now she wanted nothing more that instant than to feed Ian feet first into a meat grinder. She thought about taking Daniel's body out of there, but something told her that she shouldn't. She didn't know if Ian was close by or if he might come back. The game was still on. Why else stage all of it if not to provoke her? How could he even be sure she would find it, or was it all some sick trophy room to him?

Deciding to see how much damage had really been done, she examined the first figure and recognized one of the two hunters Ian had been feeding in the utility building. Then she found poor Caleb, apples still in his pockets. Janiss didn't even recognize most of the others. The cop didn't seem to be there; even that might have been too daring.

When did Ian have time to do all of it? Did he have to go to ground at all?

Not surprisingly, all of them had been drained of blood. She wondered if Ian had also lied about whose blood she had actually consumed.

Turning back at Daniel, she took a closer look at the bible on the podium. She finally recognized it as one of her Gramma's old family bibles, giving her yet another reason to pluck Ian's eyes out and stick untwisted wire coat hangers into his ears. A folded piece of paper was resting on the Old Testament page. She picked it up to see what it was, then noticed the chapter title.

The Book of Daniel.

Motherfucker.

The paper was a printout of a paid reservation to Stonewall Resort's dinner for Thanksgiving, dated for that evening. Ian must have found it in Daniel's things.

Daniel had bragged about taking care of Thanksgiving dinner, that he was taking Janiss someplace special. The plan was to dress up and make an evening of it, but Janiss didn't know where he'd planned to take her. She had visited the resort before, and it was a beautiful venue. It would have been a beautiful evening, too, for just the two of them.

She wanted to say something to Daniel, but she couldn't bring herself to look at him.

Why was there only one confirmation?

Because Ian had the other one.

Maybe he was leaving the area and maybe he wasn't; but if he had the other invite, he intended to use it. What was he planning to do?

Janiss looked around the church again at all of the bodies. Her muscles tensed.

She wasn't going let the prick get away with *any* of it.

Chapter 36

The alarm on her phone went off.

Janiss reached up out of her shallow grave and touched the screen to silence it. An extension cord under the cellar door had kept her phone fully charged all day. She carefully pulled it down to prevent yanking the cord out so she wouldn't have to move too much.

It was five o' clock.

The alarm had been set for earlier, but she saw it had cycled several times without waking her. Apparently, she woke whenever she was going to wake up and not a moment sooner.

She would never get used to her heart not beating until after the sun went down.

The light of day was still trickling in through the small cellar window. It was too soon. She tried not to move, watching the clock on the phone as the seconds ticked away. That was what it felt like to be dead and aware, the empty moments before the sunset.

At four minutes after five, she felt her heart lurch and begin to rhythmically beat. Her breathing resumed on its own and everything began to feel normal again.

She felt energized from her day's sleep, but the thirst she woke with was no less intense for it. There was also no time to hunt down trespassing hunters for a quick bite and she was counting on her thirst to keep her sharp.

Janiss showered quickly and abbreviated her hair routine from the night before. She was going to need more than eyeliner and base, and that was going to take the longest. After finishing her face, she opened the smaller suitcase she had brought in last Saturday and set out the contents. She took a moment to lament these things were supposed to have been for a special evening with a special someone. They still were; but with a very different intent and a very different someone.

After her unmentionables, as her Gramma used to call them, Janiss carefully slipped the one-piece outfit over her head, untwisted it to fit correctly and took a step back to see herself in the mirror.

A little black dress. A classic.

With her hair done and evening makeup on, she looked far more adult and confident than she felt. She was a living prop, a distraction for everyone – like some local celebrity that showed up unannounced. It wasn't enough for Ian alone to take notice; she wanted everyone watching, and she wanted him to see them doing it.

A long red coat completed the look for her upcoming reveal. Her insanely high heels could wait until she arrived, but her running shoes would do for driving.

After locking up the house, she checked the time on her phone again.

Six-fifteen. Not bad.

The fastest way out to Stonewall Resort was the back way out across the Lewis County line, past the Truit's place and over to I-79. Once she got to the end of the road, it was a straight shot under the interstate and out Route 19 to the state park.

Just before she drove beneath the underpass, she took a closer look at the ramp onto the southbound lane. The curve didn't look too bad. Her Kia was top heavy and there were warnings all over her sun visors about veering too quickly and the dangers of tipping over while turning. Daniel had shown her a few things about braking into curves, accelerating out of them and turning on a dime. Above all, he had told her, don't hesitate.

Janiss reached the turn to the resort where the highway widened into a split lane. The state park was beautiful, especially with snow still on the ground, and the resort complemented the surroundings. The parking lot wasn't full; but she decided to park on the outer edges of it, away from any other vehicles that might be in the way. She angled her car so she could pull straight out and no other vehicles could block her in.

She changed shoes, slipping on the heels and dropping her runners onto the backseat floor. After locking her car – the auto-lock would engage anyway if she didn't – it took her a few wobbly steps to get used to the heels again. After a moment they felt natural. It didn't hurt that she wasn't going to be wearing them for very long.

The main buildings of the resort were immense, with several wings two or three stories high of guest rooms and amenities. Rich, white walls and forest-green roofs matched all the structures and blended them well with the surroundings.

A valet service was available at the entry to the

resort, so there were service people waiting. As Janiss made her way across the parking lot and under the green roof, she was already getting looks, and that was with her coat still on. Stewards tried not to look like they were staring as she reached the automatic front doors.

"Anything I can do for you?" a nice young man in a uniform asked.

He looked delicious, and he *did* offer.

"I'm fine, thank you." Janiss grinned a little and continued inside. She bit her lip after she was past him and put his thin and easily pierced flesh out of her mind.

While the exterior was white and green, the interior of the resort was all stained wood as far as the eye could see. It looked like they skipped Thanksgiving for the next holiday; four huge Christmas trees decorated the main lobby, complete with a roaring fire. Wreaths, holly and every decoration imaginable filled every corner and crevice. There were many people, all older than she, moving about here and there. She had just turned toward the check-in desk when another wide-eyed youth made eye contact with her. The green nametag on his matching vest read "Carl" in all white letters.

"I have a paid reservation for dinner tonight," Janiss said sweetly, showing the edge of the printout. "I'm meeting someone."

"They're hosting the Thanksgiving buffet at Stillwater's Restaurant. Just show the reservation and you'll be seated."

"Can you show me where it is?"

"Absolutely, ma'am. This way."

Janiss followed Carl to the restaurant. It was huge, with tables everywhere and food for the taking. The natural-looking stained wood from the lobby was featured prominently there as well, while the chairs looked they were built out of pieces of tree limbs collected from the local forest.

It was a good-sized crowd, but not too full, mostly made up of families and couples. She noticed one particular family, a pretty couple and two young children...*very* young children. She couldn't take her eyes off them; they attracted her. She tried to tell herself it was some kind of maternal thing, but she knew it wasn't. It was more like a Hansel and Gretel thing.

One of the little boys with an empty plate wandered away from his preoccupied parents and walked directly up to Janiss. He stared at her with huge blue eyes. She could see a vein in his temple pulsing with each heartbeat.

"Are you here for dinner, too?" the boy asked.

Ian. She was there for Ian.

Focus, damn it.

Putting the little juice pouch out of her mind – she had imagined a straw taped to the little boy's back for convenience – Janiss glanced around, but didn't see Ian anywhere. The family thing didn't seem like his style. Sure, the reservation gave him the idea and got him in the door; but he couldn't be himself there. He liked tall women, he liked movies and he liked...

Whiskey.

Carl was still there, as if waiting for something. She

caught him sizing her up as she turned around, staring hard as if someone had stapled hundred-dollar bills to her coat. Had she really changed so much in just a few days that people couldn't look away? Even the little boy seemed drawn to her.

"Is there a bar around here?" Janiss asked.

Carl smiled politely and appeared in no way embarrassed for leering at her. "We have a lounge," he said, as if it was important to make the distinction. "TJ Muskies."

That had to be it. "I think I'm supposed to meet someone there."

"Right this way," he offered.

TJ Muskies was all man-cave. The fully stocked bar presided over a room filled with dark brown wood and black edging. A sizable covered fire pit in the center was the main attraction after the alcohol. Leather accents and a maze of intimate seating completed the setting along with actual candles burning inside imperfect red glass holders. Along the outer edge of the lounge were smaller fireplaces as well.

Everyone in the lounge seemed to be paired up, whether it was a couple of businessmen having a drink or lovers having an intimate moment. It wasn't very full, but the sparse emptiness added to the intimacy of the atmosphere.

As she suspected, there was Ian.

Next to a wall close to one of the smaller fireplaces, Ian sat comfortably wearing a pinstriped suit with a black shirt; the buttons down the front of the shirt were undone too far. There was a blonde perched next to him, poured into a festive green dress that was shorter than hers. It wouldn't have been so bad if it weren't for the oversized matching bow doubling as a belt that made the woman look like a cheap Christmas present. She appeared infatuated with Ian's rugged features and supreme overconfidence.

Janiss undid her coat and let it slide off her shoulders. Unasked, Carl caught it for her and folded it over his arm before she moved across the lounge. One by one, men and women both took notice of her as she fixed her eyes on her target. Both Ian and his future victim looked up and noticed her at the same time; the look of surprise on his face and of defeat on hers said it all.

Ian's eyes drifted from her shoes up to her eyes. "Well, hello..."

"Annette," Janiss offered.

"Annette," Ian acknowledged, already looking interested in whatever game Janiss was playing. He indicated the woman next to him. "This is Charlotte."

"Hello, Charlotte," Janiss said, pleasant and polite, before turning back to Ian.

"What brings you out this evening? Just in for a quick drink?"

Janiss narrowed her eyes at him. "Mother sends her regards, along with her continued disappointment."

Charlotte looked toward Ian with a puzzled and accusing look. Others were also taking notice, sensing a scene was playing out.

Janiss knew Ian didn't like being singled out, and certainly not by a woman. The look on his face told her she was under his skin already; but he neither confirmed nor condemned the accusation, something that didn't seem to be sitting well with Charlotte.

"Also," Janiss added, "she said I should ask why you beat her best friend bloody and left her for dead."

The lack of denial from Ian was enough for Charlotte. She promptly emptied her drink into his face and stormed off for show, but Janiss could tell she looked disturbed by the entire conversation.

"Are you through?" Ian asked, dabbing his face with a cloth napkin.

Janiss smiled and stepped into his reach, then let her hand fly across his face. She extended her talons as she raked him, drawing blood again from his cheek.

His control was waning – she could sense it. His fingers twitched as if he didn't know what to do with his hands. Managing an air of calm, Ian managed to set his napkin aside and leaned forward to stand up, presumably to put himself on equal ground instead of having to look up at her and undermine his ego.

Janiss recalled the night before last when she had asked Ian about fighting. His advice was to strike first and hit hard.

Ian was over-balanced as he leaned forward out of his chair. The fireplace to the side was perfectly angled from the seat he had chosen, giving her a unique opportunity. If Ian had been ready for it or she weren't a vampire, she wouldn't have the weight or strength to move him. Taking a step to his side opposite the fireplace, she shifted her weight and slammed into him with her shoulder as hard as she could.

Ian tumbled headfirst into the hearth.

The fire roared up as his head knocked over the stack of smoldering logs and hot embers spilled everywhere. The room erupted in screams and people began to scatter. Ian started to twist and flail in desperation to get out of the fireplace, rolling back out onto the floor.

Janiss reminded herself of his final piece of advice, the only real defense against another vampire she had little chance to defeat.

Run like hell.

Chapter 37

Janiss snatched her coat away from Carl as she ran for the door, only then realizing that her heels weren't going to work. Plucking them off to run barefoot, she dashed back down the hallway toward the main desk as fast as she could.

Sliding into the lobby past the front desk, the attendants behind it looked concerned. Janiss stopped for a moment, deciding on whether or not she should warn them; but anyone who got in Ian's way would probably be killed. Since she had stopped, of course, everyone looked at her as if they expected she was going to say something.

"Um...I think I left my car running."

She took a quick glance down the hall that she had just come from, but didn't see Ian. That was a good thing, she told herself. She had no idea how fast he was on foot, and it might have been too late by the time she did see him.

As she dashed across the parking lot to her car, it dawned on her that she wasn't winded. Why should she be? She didn't have to breathe. She fumbled to unlock the vehicle, throwing her coat and heels into the back before scolding herself that neither of them was important enough to have carried all that way.

Janiss jumped into the seat, turned the key to start

the car and pulled out into the roadway before checking her rearview mirror. She expected a commotion at the front door, or at least to see Ian running after her. Had she completely miscalculated how much of an egotistical murdering misogynist he was?

The engine roar of a Cadillac Escalade pierced the night, the front end barreling up over the hill from a lower parking lot. The high-intensity headlamps glowed a brilliant blue at the edges and made the massive SUV seem to scowl at her like some black steel demon.

So far, so good. Well, "successful" – "good" felt a little off.

Janiss put her Kia into drive and stomped on the gas. She had to make the right turn onto Route 19 before he caught up to her and put some distance between them before turning onto the interstate. The faster she got to the Burnsville exit, the better off she'd be. The hairpin turns would force Ian to slow down, giving her a better chance to stay ahead of him all the way to Cedarcrest.

Time to make a call.

Chapter 38

The phone rang on Timothy's cell. The call transferred to his computer in Louisa's office.

"Cedarcrest Found–"

"Timothy!" Janiss cut him off. "I found Ian!"

Timothy opened a new window on his desktop and clicked a saved link. A map was generated with a blue dot moving across it. The vehicle was on the interstate and heading in a southwesterly direction.

"Timothy?" Janiss shouted again. "Did you hear me? Stupid network..."

"I'm here," he confirmed. "Judging from your tone, I assume he's right behind you?"

"He's chasing me. I kind of pissed him off."

"That might not have been the best of ideas," Timothy pointed out.

Louisa leaned in close over the desk. "Can you lead him here?"

"I think so. That was the plan, right?"

Timothy looked up at Louisa. She nodded.

"By the way," Janiss added, "after what I found yesterday, I'm completely on board with whatever you have planned for the bastard."

"Just get here," Timothy said. "We'll be ready."

"Any advice while I'm running for my life?"

Louisa answered. "Don't stop."

Chapter 39

Janiss had shot past the rest area a little over halfway to the Burnsville exit. Twice she had seen the blue tinged headlights in her rearview mirror after going over another hill. Her gas tank was mostly full thanks to Timothy; but the curvy mountain interstate highway wasn't designed for speeds in excess of eighty-five miles an hour. Flashing warning signs appeared after every hilltop about low grades, gearing down and excessive speed.

She had passed several cars already, happy none of them were police. That was one of the things she hadn't thought through: what would happen if the cops got in on the chase?

Janiss checked her mirrors again. The road was dark behind her. She was relieved Ian hadn't caught up to her yet but worried he might give up. Her headlights flashed on mile marker 82. She was almost to Burnsville.

Then she heard an engine roar, too loud to be her own. The lights of a vehicle almost next to her flashed on. Ian had been driving with his lights off and had slid up right beside her.

Something struck the side of her car, busting out the driver's side window. The glass fell out completely, most of it stuck to the plastic tint. Janiss looked over to see the passenger door of the Escalade missing. Ian was straddling the front bucket seats with his left hand on the wheel. He must have been driving with the cruise control on so he could slide across the seat and kick his door off.

He *kicked* his door off.

"Hey, Janiss!" Ian screamed over the wind rushing past the window. "Pull over! I wanna rip your heart out!"

He was playing with her.

She could play, too.

Janiss jerked her wheel and crashed her Kia into the side of the Escalade. She didn't hit it hard – but with his cruise control active and only one hand that could still reach the wheel, Ian couldn't correct for the collision and started to lose control of the vehicle. The Escalade turned out of the left lane and scraped against the concrete divider of the overpass, quickly slowing down until he could recover.

Was it his *door* that had shattered her window?

As the blue-tinged lights fell back behind her, the Exit 79 sign loomed ahead: "Route 5, Burnsville Glenville." She hoped Ian would miss the exit and have to turn around. Either way, she knew she had a better chance staying ahead of him on the state road than on the open interstate.

Slowing down just enough to blow through the stop sign at the end of the off ramp, Janiss laughed a little at the "Speed Limit 35 MPH" sign as she passed it on the straightaway doing sixty. Crossing the railroad tracks after the road narrowed back into a simple divided two-lane, she passed another sign that indicated it was seventeen miles to Glenville.

No problem. She wasn't going that far.

Chapter 40

Another car on the interstate had cut Ian off after Janiss's hit and run, making him miss the exit ramp before the overpass. With a quick glance over his shoulder, he jerked the Escalade across both lanes and turned the vehicle down the on-ramp, narrowly missing another car coming up the other way.

Ian couldn't stop smiling about the look of horror on Janiss's face when his car door slammed into hers!

She had intrigued him from the moment he saw her, but that had mostly been a physical attraction: she looked delicious. While quizzing her about what she was doing at Cedarcrest, he'd lucked into discovering Sarah's likely intent to make her.

Why would she decide to create another vampire after all that time?

Asking Sarah directly wouldn't have been any fun, so he turned Janiss himself and hadn't been disappointed. Sure, Sarah had sent her back to the house; but he was fairly certain Janiss wasn't told to go out into the backyard and badmouth her killer. Even after he'd knocked her across the yard for taking a swipe at him, she still didn't back down.

Janiss obviously found the invitation he'd left for her at the church, but he never imagined she would confront him while he was on the prowl. She even openly attacked him! That must completely have been Janiss's idea. Sarah wouldn't have suggested it, any more than she would have considered doing it herself.

Ian had looked for someone like Sarah for years: a strong and independent woman who could blossom from an infusion of power. It didn't bother him that Sarah hated him for doing it; it was that she had rejected the gift he'd given her and chose to see it as a curse. Even that would have been forgivable if she would have just left him alone after driving him off. Her meek little house wench served as a fine example of what Sarah could expect if she continued to cross him.

And then there was Janiss.

The moment "Annette" walked into that lounge, she was a vision. Every eye in the room was drawn to her confidence and stride. Any of the cattle grazing there would have happily fed themselves to her if she had only asked, just to be in her presence a little while longer before their pathetic lives bled out of them. Poor Charlotte had been destroyed before a single word was uttered.

Looking ahead down the road into the darkness, Ian recognized the taillights of Janiss's Kia just before she turned the corner. She must have floored it the moment she turned onto the straightaway to get so far ahead of him. He was beginning to imagine she enjoyed being chased more than being caught; her little boyfriend could have suffered his entire lifetime never figuring that out. The poor guy was better off as he was: a corpse tied to a podium inside an abandoned house of hypocrisy.

Janiss, however, had another thing coming.

She was leading him to Cedarcrest, where "Louisa" was waiting to do *whatever* to him. Once he disposed of that loose end, he would deal with Janiss. Breaking both of her legs, dragging her back to her Gramma's house, and tossing her into the cellar again seemed appropriate.

It was the principle of the thing. She'd understand.

Hot embers in the eyes hurt, damn it.

Chapter 41

Janiss started thinking about how Ian had caught up to her with his lights off. It seemed dangerous – but could she do that, too?

After passing a slow old Chevy, Janiss switched her headlights down to the parking light setting. She widened her pupils and focused ahead, seeing everything the way she did back in the woods behind the farmhouse. Turning her lights off completely and dimming the dashboard to nothing made it even better. It didn't feel like she was driving; it felt like she was flying over the road at night.

There was a flash of light behind her. She checked quickly, thinking Ian had already caught up. Nothing was back there, not even Ian running with his lights off. It looked like a camera flash, only brighter.

It couldn't have been lightning, could it?

Wisps of fog appeared across the road in front of her. The wind across her open window began to howl. Two more flashes appeared behind her. She glanced into her mirror by the time the second flash went off, seeing the tell-tale pattern of a lightning strike a second before the thunder sounded.

A blinding arc of lightning flashed onto the ground in front of her car as the accompanying thunderclap deafened her. Janiss gripped the wheel in a desperate attempt to keep control of the car, resisting the urge to turn and avoid something that disappeared an instant after. Vampire or not, it ruined her night vision and there were some serious curves coming up.

Janiss switched her lights back on and blinked her eyes back to normal. The fog was already so heavy that the headlights reflected too much light as she passed through various patches of mist.

She pressed the call button on her steering wheel, letting the voice prompts guide her to place a call to Timothy. She had to yell over the wind coming though her missing window.

"How are you faring, Ms. Connelly?" Timothy asked.

"No time for bullshit!" she snapped. "Can vampires control the weather? Like, create fog or call down lighting?"

Another bolt flashed just off her right bumper, a sheet of brilliance across her windshield, closer than before. The second thunderclap echoed in her ears. For a few moments, she couldn't hear anything before the wind at her window became clear again. Somewhere in the darkness behind her she heard tires squealing, but couldn't see any lights in her mirror. Ian couldn't have been very far back.

Why the hell wasn't Timothy answering her?

The speakers inside the Kia played the incoming call ring tone.

The call had dropped; Timothy was calling her back. "The answer is yes."

Janiss winced. "Well, what happens if it hits my car?"

"It's mostly a distraction. Some electrical systems might ground out, or it may do nothing at all. As long as you're not touching any bare metal, it shouldn't hurt you."

"*Shouldn't?*" she hissed. "Are you *sure*?"

Timothy sighed. "No."

"Well...shit!" Janiss gripped the steering wheel in frustration before realizing she might be strong enough to rip it off.

"You're coming up on Sand Fork soon, yes?"

Janiss thought about that. "Timothy, did Louisa Lo-Jack my car?"

Timothy ignored the question. "Can you stay ahead of him, Janiss?"

Janiss sighed. "I think so. I'm pretty sure he doesn't know the road like I do."

"Once you hit Butcher's Run over the bridge, it's a straight line up the road to Cedarcrest. The gate will be open. Park as close as you can and run for the door, but don't come in until you see that he has seen you. Do *not* stop on the seal in front of the doors. After he sees you, come inside and go straight to the back of the lobby. Once you're in the middle elevator, you'll be safe. The door will open for you."

"Then what happens?"

"You'll see."

The phone clicked off.

Chapter 42

Janiss worried Ian might catch up to her before she reached Sand Fork, but no one was behind her. There was a curious lack of any traffic at all, but maybe that was just good luck. Following one more hard right turn, it was almost a straight shot all the way up to the Butcher's Run bridge.

No sooner than she had cleared the turn than she saw Ian flip on his lights and heard his engine roar. Was he going to ram her? Janiss floored it, but the tachometer jumped into the red with little improvement in actual speed.

The Escalade rear-ended her, propelling her forward. With both hands on the steering wheel she managed not to spin or flip the vehicle, but she had come very close. Up ahead was a street lamp that illuminated the edge of the bridge and the road widened into a split turn lane. She was about to miss the turn and it would be unlikely Ian would give her a second chance to turn around.

Janiss quickly changed lanes to the right as she lightly pulled back on her parking brake. Ian didn't slow down and vaulted around her, his brake lights brightening as he shot past the turn. Janiss cut her steering wheel left and accelerated. The rear brakes didn't lock up, allowing her a somewhat-controlled sideways skid across the split lane that lined her up in the correct direction across the bridge. Releasing the parking brake, she stomped on her gas pedal.

It wasn't pretty, but Daniel would have approved.

After passing the turn to the prison, it only took about a minute before she could see the street lights illuminating the turnaround at the end of the road and the right turn up to Cedarcrest. Before she could even take her foot off the gas to brake, a thick fog came down on her like a snow bank instantly obscuring everything – immediately followed by a series of lightning bolts crashing down onto the Kia.

She gripped the steering wheel to keep control of the car instead of covering her ears from the thunderclaps, but it didn't matter. Her instrument panel flared, flickered and darkened. The engine died along with the power steering. She finally stepped on the brake, but there was almost no pressure. She might as well have put her feet through the floorboards to stop.

Blind, out of control and still going too fast, Janiss pulled the parking brake again, yanking too hard and causing the rear wheels to slide out. She tried to guess when to make the turn through the gate, but the car crashed into the left side of the gatehouse instead.

Janiss focused, reeling but aware. Nothing seemed broken and she didn't want to know what being inside of a car rammed by an Escalade would feel like. Janiss tried the driver's door, but it was pinned on that side.

Blue-tinged headlights flashed in the distance as the fog dissipated, letting Janiss see for an instant that the gate was opened as promised. She straddled the gearshift and tried the passenger door, opening it easily. Scooting over the seats, Janiss sprinted barefoot over the gate threshold, clearing the metal grating across the road. It was still too far to the doors as the SUV roared up behind her. She held her breath, fully expecting to be run down.

She heard a sound like a trash dumpster impacting the ground after being dropped off a building. Janiss stopped and everything went quiet. Surprised she was unhurt and untouched, she turned to look. A barrier had been raised from beneath the grating after Janiss had crossed it, and the Escalade had slammed into it head on. Whether the airbag failed to deploy or had already deployed earlier, Ian had been thrown through his windshield and clear of the wreck.

He was getting back up, too, and she didn't like how much closer he already was to her.

Janiss ran for the door, up the ramp, over the seal and stopped just inside. The glass doors closed normally like any other time, as if unaware of any urgency. She looked across the lobby, finding the red lights illuminated and the inside doors closed.

The central elevator was not open.

What? Why?

Then she remembered. Ian needed to see her.

Standing inside the glass doors and looking out, Janiss could see Ian wasn't exactly running. He looked like she felt. They *had* just both been in a car wreck.

Ian then looked up, noticed her and grinned wickedly.

The moment he stepped across the circular seal, what she assumed to be a wooden spear shot up through one of the goggle-eyes of the fang faces carved into it. The spear was at least Ian's height fully extended, narrowly missing impaling him on it. When Ian stepped again, another one sprang up, forcing him to step back to avoid it.

Ian's eyes were dark and his facial muscles swelled. With his fangs bared, he looked every bit like the monster he was. His expression was equal parts maniacal and insane.

Grabbing hold of one of the spears, he smashed his fist through the base of it to break it off, then hurled it toward the glass barrier in front of Janiss. The tip pierced the glass of the doors and stopped, suspended halfway through by the plastic tint in the window. Behind her, she finally heard the wonderful chime of the central elevator door opening.

Thank God.

Janiss dashed across the lobby and almost fell into the elevator in desperation to get inside. She pressed the Door Close and third floor buttons, but neither responded. Looking up and hoping to find one of those little black camera dots, she spotted one and looked horrified into it.

"Timothy?" she said with a frightened tone.

Outside, she could see Ian still making his way through the minefield of stakes. He was almost through them and he had little in the way of any damage to show for it. When he reached the doors, he pulled out the spear and brutally beat his way through the safety glass.

"Timothy!" Janiss screamed.

Just as Ian stepped through the doorway and spotted her in the elevator across the lobby, the door closed.

Chapter 43

The elevator door opened on the third floor. The lights were on inside Louisa's office.

Janiss took her time walking down the hall, taking a few moments for herself. After all of the running, driving and more running, she just wanted to sit down and everything to stop. Ian was there, she did her part – and that was that.

As she peered inside the office, Timothy was seated behind the desk with both laptops open and watching some kind of video feeds on them. Sensing Janiss was there, he pointed at a tall black coffee mug sitting on one of the side workstation counter tops.

Janiss gratefully went to it and cupped it in her hands, then stopped herself. She looked back to Timothy, who ,at that moment, was looking directly at her.

"Did you already feed tonight?" he asked, sounding curious.

"No," she answered with a suspicious tone. "How much longer were you going to dangle me as bait?"

"As long as it took and not much longer." Timothy looked at the mug in Janiss's hands, then back at her. "I would really prefer if you drank that."

Without taking so much as a sip, Janiss set the mug down exactly where she found it. "Where's Louisa?"

"Janiss, please."

"You said I'd find out when I got here, so tell me already. I think I've earned it."

Timothy turned the laptop around. The screen was showing a closeup of Ian in the elevator.

Janiss shuddered. "He's not coming up here, is he?"

"*Down there*," Timothy corrected.

Similar to when she first rode in that elevator car, the concealed back door opened when it reached the bottom floor. Ian found himself in the dark hallway of doors, but the metallic one at the end was wide open. There was a light coming from inside the room and someone was standing there waiting for him.

"Is that Louisa? What is she going to do?"

"I've been told she intends to 'beat him down.'"

"Can she? Beat him, I mean?"

Ian took his time walking the length of the hallway. The moment he stepped into the room at the end, the door rose up and sealed the room shut. Timothy closed the laptop and looked back at Janiss.

"That's it?" she asked. "What happens now?"

"Whatever happens in that room, Ian will be taken care of. It's no longer your concern."

"What about Louisa? What if she can't defeat him?"

Timothy didn't respond, but he looked saddened at the thought.

"Show me what's going on in there, Timothy." Janiss met his eyes and tried to compel him. "Do it — *now.*"

Timothy stared back, composed and unmoving.

Huh?

"I know I'm not doing this wrong," she said, "and I know you're not a vampire. How are you...?"

"I'm a ghoul," he explained. "Just like the residents, Louisa feeds me a little of her blood every other day. Among other things, it makes me immune to your thrall."

"Does it make you immune to me ripping out your throat?"

She could tell that the threat worried him; but it was a hollow threat and she felt bad for even saying it. His eyes drifted to the unemptied coffee mug across the room, then again back to her.

Janiss retrieved the mug, drained it and set it down again. It was the first time she had satisfied her thirst that she wasn't consumed by it. There were other things on her mind that were more important, and she didn't want to see Louisa destroyed for no reason at all.

"I would never intentionally hurt you, Timothy. I'm sorry I threatened you."

"I believe you. I don't think you would knowingly hurt anyone. This is why she chose you – and you've demonstrated remarkable control in very little time. You don't allow yourself to be dominated by your craving and you have a keen focus when you choose to apply yourself. It's admirable."

Janiss was humbled but wary. "Was that an actual compliment?"

"I trust you won't tell anyone."

"And he's back."

Janiss pulled one of the workstation chairs up to the desk, seated herself, then indicated the laptop. "Are we forbidden to watch this?"

"If I let you watch, I'd like your promise that whatever happens, you'll do nothing about it and won't ask me to interfere."

Janiss didn't like it, but she nodded anyway.

Chapter 44

"Where's Janiss?" Ian asked Louisa, sizing up the round room looking for hidden traps. "I already know I can kick *your* ass, and I really want her to see what her heart looks like."

"I'm afraid it's just me, Ian. You remember – the wife you abandoned, right?"

Louisa was dressed in a dark purple *gi* with a black baton in each hand. Ian wasn't impressed.

"You should have brought stakes. The only thing those sticks are good for is whatever I can think up after I take them away from you."

"You are welcome to try, my love. Please try."

Ian began to circle the room, looking at Louisa while searching for a weakness or a reaction. "I thought you petitioned for a divorce."

"I did. It took me four years to scrape your name off of mine."

"Why are you still hung up on me after all these years?"

"You *know* why, Ian."

"You know that isn't even my real name. He was just the Happy Meal whose identity I took."

Louisa didn't look ready; but when Ian lunged at her, she twisted away and followed though with a hit on his back. Ian was surprised and even a little hurt.

"Ow. Guess you're serious about this whole 'hurting me' thing, huh?"

Louisa smirked. "I'm serious about destroying you, Ian. Beating on you is merely foreplay."

He flashed his fangs through a wicked smile, then came across the room at Louisa again. His move was the same as before, modified to account for Louisa's dodge and attack. Louisa changed it up again, landing a hit to his shoulder and a second to the side of his head. Her speed matched his.

Rubbing the side of his head where her last hit had landed, Ian paced again rethinking his strategy. "What was that little harlot's name you kept in your rooms at the boarding house? Eris? Ellen? Erica?"

"Eleanor," Louisa answered with a sour tone.

"Janiss told me you wanted to know why I beat her to death. I guess I owe you that. It's simple, really. I asked her a question and she didn't answer it, so I followed through on my threat to make her answer me."

Louisa scowled. "What was the question?"

"I asked her where you were. She said she didn't know, but we both know she just didn't want to tell me."

"She *didn't* know, Ian. I hadn't told her."

"Now, see? I just assumed she was protecting you, so what was I supposed to do? All she did was put her arms up and cry, trying to keep me from hitting her in the face. Well, until I broke both of her arms, then it was just a lot of crying. I thought of you every time I drew back my fist – so you can see how it was all just a big misunderstanding. Why can't you just forgive me?"

Louisa moved in, swinging wildly with both batons. Ian stepped inside their reach, shielding him from her swing while allowing him to claw at her abdomen several times before she could get away from him.

Her body language changed. On the defensive, she kept her wounds away from him, watching Ian with her head twisted at an awkward angle. Ian felt no worse than when he got up after being thrown from the Escalade and had recovered nicely.

"What did you call this again, my love?" Ian chided. "Foreplay? I was going suggest we should invite Janiss in for a *menage à trois.*"

Chapter 45

Janiss was sickened by what she was seeing.

Louisa already looked hurt and it seemed as though her heart was no longer in the fight. How else could it end but with Louisa dying alone?

"Let me in there," Janiss commanded Timothy.

"You promised."

"I didn't promise anything, I nodded. Maybe..."

"Maybe you'll what?"

"I can help." Or die trying, she thought.

Timothy focused back on the screens. "You would be a distraction to her. She would try to protect you, then you would both be destroyed."

"Better than her suffering like this and then being destroyed."

Timothy turned to Janiss and put his hand on her arm, probably the most intimate thing she had seen him do. "If you believe in what Louisa was trying to do here, you know we have to protect the source. You, Janiss. She wouldn't be in there if she didn't know you were safe out here."

A drop of blood formed in the corner of her eye. "That's why I can't let her. It's wrong."

"What about the other folks in the private wing? Ruth, John, Vivian? How long do you think they'll last if their source is gone? It can't be stored, and it expires very quickly. It's mystical."

Janiss looked angrily at him. "How long have you worked here, Timothy? For her?"

He didn't answer.

"Is silence how you always answer tough questions, or just how you avoid the truth?"

The accusation irritated him. "Your 'truth' is what's in your heart, not in your head. The reason I have been trusted with the facility access codes and not you is because she knows I'll do what's right and not act on how I feel."

Timothy was passionate about his dedication to the Foundation, Janiss could tell, but in spite of everything he was saying, he wasn't sold on sacrificing Louisa for it. He projected his professional persona like a shield, like someone who had been hurt and didn't want to be hurt again. Before Ian, she probably wouldn't have been able to relate.

Still, in spite of his protests to the contrary, Timothy had also slipped up.

"Access codes?" she asked.

Chapter 46

It was true. Louisa had underestimated Ian's ferocity.

Once she had built Cedarcrest and her rooms beneath the walking garden, the training room was where she spent every spare moment. It was where she trained, thought up strategies and practiced them.

There hadn't been anyone to practice against, of course. She didn't know any other vampires and certainly not one of indeterminable age who could take strength from his rage with no discernible weakness. She guessed Ian hadn't fed for the night and had suffered not only a car accident, but several wounds from the spears outside.

None of it affected him. If he was hurt or slowing down, she couldn't see it – or he was better than her at not showing it. Louisa felt strong at the beginning of the fight, hitting first and appearing to have the upper hand. That had all changed and she wasn't sure if she could regain it.

Her doubts poisoned her while his overconfidence made him strong. She would have despised him for that alone even if there had been nothing else.

Ian started to circle Louisa, using her round room against her. There were no defensible corners, a feature meant to keep Ian from getting away; but he had turned that against her. He came at her at random, in his own time; and all she could do was defend herself, one attack at a time.

He was clever – ensuring that anything more than defense would overextend her, and then he could take her at will. Twice he had passed up the opportunity to take her weapons away, perhaps thinking that letting her keep them would make her feel more useless than she already did.

It was a waiting game now.

Louisa knew Ian was trapped and had already made provisions to destroy him, but it still wasn't enough. She wanted him to suffer, to know it was by her hand that it had happened, to take that personal power back from him after all these years. It was a different world then and, in some ways, Ian still lived there.

She had a single strategy left, but it wasn't going to be pleasant.

Chapter 47

"No," Timothy answered again.

Janiss frowned. "You can open doors, move elevators around and enable security systems...and you're telling me you can't get me down there?"

"I said 'I won't.'" There was finality in his statement.

Irritated at his refusals, Janiss turned the monitor around so he couldn't look away from it. "Look at her, Timothy. He's playing with her. It's what he does, and it's infuriating and defeating. He makes people fear him, taking their power away. Think about everything he's done."

"It's what Louisa wanted. It's why she's doing it. He's done, so she wins. Everything else is irrelevant."

"With all this high-tech stuff, you're telling me that you don't have a closet full of guns and flame throwers around here?"

"It's not about that. It wouldn't matter that way. She wants to defeat him when he thinks he can't be, when he has the upper hand."

Janiss looked desperate and frustrated. "Okay, then let me talk to her. There's gotta be a speaker into the room, right? I can tell her something inspirational."

Or something to really piss Ian off.

Timothy considered it. "There isn't a speaker into

that room. Louisa demanded silence without interruption whenever she meditated or trained. However, the room itself isn't soundproof out into the hallway. If you took the elevator down, you could talk to them safely outside of the room."

Janiss looked hopeful. It was something. Anything was better than being useless. "Will you let me?"

Timothy opened a window on one of the laptops and pressed a few keys. "Get into the elevator and I'll send you down. Once the elevator door shuts, I won't open it again until Ian is dealt with. That door is the secondary boundary. If he escapes and gets through, everyone in this facility is at risk – including your friends in the private wing. Do you understand?"

Janiss stood up, took his head in her hands and kissed his forehead. "Thanks, Timothy."

"That's not going to become a habit, is it?"

Chapter 48

The elevator stopped on the subterranean floor beneath the walking garden. Still barefoot and wearing her little black dress, it felt a little like "the walk of shame" to Janiss: coming home the next morning from a party the night before in your evening clothes. It was nothing she had ever done herself, but she could sympathize.

As promised, the back door to the elevator closed. At the end of the hallway was the featureless, metallic door that led directly into the training room. Standing in front of it, Janiss had a chance to make a difference – but had no idea what to say.

She paced in the hallway for a moment, reminding herself it could be over in an instant if Ian got bored. Okay. If she couldn't inspire Louisa, plan B was getting under Ian's skin – and that was something she already knew how to do very well.

"Hey, Ian!" Janiss screamed out. "How's it feel to know I'm right behind this door and that you'll never be able to lay a finger on me?"

She listened for a response. She heard nothing.

Nothing at all.

There should have been combat sounds or something unless it was already over. Janiss pressed her ear against the door. It was silent, not even a muffled sound escaped. It must have been completely soundproofed.

Timothy lied to her and she was trapped in the hallway outside while Louisa was inside dying.

She looked up and found one of the dot cameras above the elevator door; she hoped Timothy was watching and listening.

"Timothy, I know you can hear me! If you lied about the soundproofing, you probably lied about the speaker, too. Patch me in or something. Let them hear me! I want to talk to them!"

No response. She had badgered Timothy until he pretended to do something and now Janiss was out of sight and out of mind.

The more she thought about it, the madder she got. She let her rage out, feeling her muscles swell and her claws extend. The door was made of steel, but she dared to believe she was made of something stronger. With everything she could muster, she threw her weight into her arm and shoulder, slamming her fist into the door as hard as she could.

There wasn't so much as a scratch or dent, no evidence she had attempted to do a thing. The room had been built to keep Ian in. Why would she hope to think it couldn't keep her out?

Tears of blood started to fall from her eyes.

No one should have to die alone.

Chapter 49

"You know what I think?" Ian asked. "You never thought you could beat me at all. You never intended to."

Louisa, looking defeated, maintained her defensive posture as Ian continued to circle her like a lion just out of her reach. Her right leg had been injured and pained her to put weight on it. If she could keep Ian talking, she might recover enough to defend herself; but he already seemed well aware that he could finish her off whenever he chose – slowly, if he preferred.

Fortunately, all she had to do to keep him talking was not interrupt. With the doors sealed, Ian wasn't going to escape. Just once, she wanted to see him defeated, to feel any degree of the helplessness he inflicted upon others.

And she needed it to be at her hands.

There was still one thing left she could do, one last trick up her sleeve. It would only take a moment, but Ian appeared at the top of his game. She had no idea how old of an immortal he was or what the true height of his ability might be, but she was certain she had underestimated it. He watched her every move, already countering anything she could think of before she even had the chance to do it.

Perhaps it would be simpler to just let him rip her apart and be done with it at long last.

"I think you're still feeling guilty about Eleanor," Ian continued. "It should have been you lying in a bloody, broken heap on the floor of that boarding house. This is your way of somehow punishing yourself. I get it – and I'm glad I could help. For now, however..."

Ian lashed out again, faster than she had ever seen him. He was using her bad leg to his advantage, seeing where she had her weight set to force her off-balance. He batted away the baton in her right hand and twisted her arm up, forcing Louisa to her knees. She still had the baton in her left hand, but it was useless since she couldn't reach him with it. If she tried to move, he would likely rip her arm off and wouldn't stop there.

"Any last words, my love?" Ian asked.

248

Chapter 50

Timothy had the training room video feed displayed on one screen and Janiss on the other. Both women looked spent, Louisa physically and Janiss emotionally.

"Let it play out" was what Louisa had said. He was expressly forbidden to interfere. Janiss, however, was not what he expected. How could someone infused with a killer instinct and the natural weapons to do the job retain so much heart?

It was the reason he refused Louisa's offer himself; he had been her first choice, after all. He didn't trust himself to retain anything of his own humanity and understood that about his personality. He wasn't a cold, calculating creature – he just preferred to follow someone with a vision. The same thing he was afraid he wouldn't keep if he became a vampire was the same thing Janiss dearly held on to, in spite of everything that had happened to her.

What could be more of a distraction than that?

Timothy called up an on-screen window. A prompt asked for an override code. He keyed in the sequence, held his breath and tapped the enter key.

Let it play out.

Chapter 51

The steel door between Janiss and the training room dropped.

Ian turned his head, seeing Janiss bleeding from her eyes and looking distraught. Being the source of so much pain seemed to delight him.

"You shouldn't have!" Ian said, as though Janiss were presenting herself to him as a gift.

Janiss saw something else as he looked at her. His face relaxed for an instant, one of Ian's little moments when the bravado ended and an actual feeling for anyone other than himself poisoned him. Somewhere deep down, perhaps there was still one tiny speck of Ian Chrisman that wasn't a complete monster.

All three vampires in the room heard the tiny click.

In Louisa's left hand, a concealed switch activated a hidden spring, ejecting the metal end of the two-foot baton to expose a perfectly carved stake. The wood was almost white in contrast to the black baton. Louisa completed the twist in her arm that Ian had threatened her with, painfully wrenching it out of her socket herself to swing the weapon toward Ian. The move also pulled him down toward her, meeting his chest with the stake as she thrust it in. Louisa held onto it all the way through until her own grip stopped it from penetrating further.

The metal shaft of the baton clanged against the

ground a moment after. Ian was on his back with his heart run through by the stake and Louisa having fallen on top of him.

Ian's face was contorted in a silent scream. Janiss knew only too well what kind of pain he was in. He struggled in vain for a moment before mustering the strength to raise his right arm, his hand slowly coming up toward the stake. Louisa's face was down, as if she were solely concentrating on keeping the stake in place with her left hand.

Janiss gasped, afraid he might actually pull it out. She saw Louisa let go of the stake. In disbelief, she tried to cry out a warning.

Louisa grabbed Ian's wrist.

One of the other two steel doors dropped open. Louisa's security guys, Travis and Cole, rushed in with clanging duffel bags while two other large men wheeled in a hospital gurney. After helping Louisa to her feet, they removed all manner of shackles from the bags and began to secure Ian, including an unusual-looking apparatus that appeared to hold the stake in place to prevent any accidental or intentional removal. Once their task was completed, Ian was lifted onto the gurney and wheeled out of the room.

Janiss approached Louisa cautiously. By the way Louisa held her arm, she must have been in excruciating pain.

"Satisfied?" Janiss asked.

"Almost. Timothy needs a good talking to about following directions, but I'll leave that for the new administrator to deal with. Do you think you'll keep him on?"

Janiss had her arms up, but looked as if she didn't know what to do with them.

"What's wrong, child?"

"I want to hug you, but I don't want to hurt you. It's kind of frustrating."

"Go ahead. I couldn't possibly be in any more pain."

Janiss threw her arms around her. Louisa must have tried not to show how much more it hurt or how wrong she had been that it wouldn't have; but Janiss felt her tense and realized she had endured it all the same.

"What happens now?" Janiss asked. She couldn't stop crying and noticed that her nose was bleeding, too. "It's kind of horrible that you can't have a good cry without looking like a plague victim."

"Then save it for special occasions, dear. What happens now is that I supervise Ian's disposal and things go back to normal."

"And by supervise, you mean...?"

"Personally."

Janiss shook her head. "Why? Just live."

"I died over a hundred years ago. I was in my fifties already. Isn't a century and a half enough?"

"Not if it was in fear of someone like *him*."

Louisa smiled. "This wasn't about that. I wanted him to feel the anguish he caused in others. It won't matter if it doesn't affect him. He won't have time to forget it."

"He'll laugh this off like everything else."

"That may change in a few minutes. We'll see."

"A few minutes? You're doing whatever it is right now? Weren't you even going to say goodbye?"

"I am, Janiss. This is goodbye."

Chapter 52

It resembled the inside of an iron lung, Ian thought – or at least what he expected the inside of one to look like.

The shackles were overkill. As he had told Janiss, there wasn't anything a vampire could do to un-stake themselves once they were impaled. He was impressed with the stake fitting, though: a system of end caps and chain links that kept the wood through his chest and not able to fall through or out.

Clever.

Ian was on his back and perfectly secured. Tiny lights beamed down to illuminate the interior. He hadn't been destroyed or buried yet, so he guessed Louisa had some kind of gloat session in mind before dropping him into a hole or whatever.

The end of the capsule opened and someone was crawling in on top of him: Louisa. After she was fully inside, the door was resealed. It looked difficult for her with her right arm in a sling, but she managed to make it up to his eye level and propped herself up on her left arm.

"Comfortable?" she asked him.

"I did have something I wanted to get off my chest," Ian whispered.

Louisa smiled fondly at him. "Besides me?"

Ian grinned. "I'm trying to be serious."

"Since when? Your ability to enjoy life after death has

long been your only positive attribute. If only there was a way to cut the rest away — but then you wouldn't be you."

"It sounds like you're fawning over me. Didn't you come here to gloat?"

"I'm supervising," Louisa said. "I like to ensure that everything at my facility runs smoothly and that everyone is taken care of."

"Well, then, I appreciate the attention. How will you be taking care of me?"

"In less than ninety seconds, the gas nozzles underneath you will open and the igniters will fire. You're in a custom-built, medical-waste-grade incinerator I had built especially for you."

"What are you doing in here, then?"

Louisa smiled and titled her head at him. "I told you. I'm supervising."

Ian tried in vain to turn his head. "You're staying in here? With me?"

"Does that bother you, my love?"

Yes, it bothered him. She'd won and he'd lost. That's not how it was supposed to work!

"Why would you do that?" he asked.

"Maybe I'm tired. Maybe I want to see what comes next, or maybe I just want to make sure you're wiped off the face of the earth."

"You still believe in an afterlife?" Ian chuckled. "After everything you've seen? Everything you know?"

"We can find out together in about a minute."

It was all wrong. How could she still cling to a creation myth and be what she was?

"Sarah, I'm sorry."

Louisa tried not to laugh. "You're apologizing? The great Ian Chrisman is sorry? I hold out hope that there's something more beyond this life and you suddenly feel the need to make last minute amends? That's guilt talking, Ian. Are you certain you believe what you think you believe?"

"There can't be a God and let things like us exist. It's all bullshit."

"Faith isn't foolish, Ian. Maybe the old men who make up rules and pass judgment have corrupted the intent, but not everyone goes through this life inflicting themselves on others. It's comforting to know that something better lies ahead for those who tried to live well and penance awaits those who exist only to make others miserable."

Ian was at a loss for words.

"Thirty seconds," Louisa reminded him.

Was he really sorry? There were no penalties, no consequences, nothing to answer for in life or death. He wasn't sorry, but he was impressed that Sarah could get under his skin one more time – even if that time was almost up.

"I think I still love you, Sarah Linn," Ian said, and meant it.

The lights over their heads blinked out and a hissing sound came from underneath them.

"To my eternal shame," Louisa replied.

There was a ticking sound...

...and all that remained of their world together was engulfed in searing flames.

Chapter 53

It was three in the morning on Black Friday.

Janiss tried not to laugh. At least her dress matched the occasion.

She had cried herself empty just after midnight and had been sitting alone by the windows in Louisa's office looking out at the gate. A wrecker was pulling Ian's Escalade off of the barrier. Her faithful, but totaled, Kia was already up on a flatbed.

Timothy came in through the open office door and set some paperwork on the desk. Janiss looked over and smiled at him as best she could. She thought he might be more affected by what had just happened, but he seemed as professional as ever.

He noticed her after a moment. "I like your dress."

Janiss turned her back to look out the windows again. He could have at least said it with more enthusiasm.

"Your predecessor used to spend hours looking out those windows," he added after a moment, shuffling and sorting through his paperwork.

That sounded depressing. "Looks like I'm already following in her footsteps."

"You may be taking her place; but you're under no obligation to become her, Janiss. Believe me. I drew up the contracts myself."

"I know," Janiss replied, appreciating his attempt at humor. "The sad part is that I'm beginning to see everything she saw, feel what she was feeling. I don't like this or where it led – and I don't want to turn out like her."

"You're *not* like her."

Janiss decided she'd try to stop feeling sorry for herself for a while. "Did you tell the police about the church?"

"Our liaison at the sheriff's office is looking into it now. It appears that this may have been a copycat killing. The perpetrator was killed on site at Locust Knob."

"That's a lie," Janiss whispered.

"The body of Daniel Moore will also be found among them, one of the nine victims. His parents will know what happened and will have a body they can bury."

"Another lie. I was the one responsible." She looked out the window, seeing her old car disappear past the gate as the tow truck pulled away. She remembered that she had forgotten Ruth's gift still in the car.

"Did you want to confess and serve the next thirty-years-to-life next door? Plenty of free time and all you can eat."

The statement was horrific, but Janiss still found herself grinning as she turned toward him. "I can't believe you just said that."

"If it makes you feel any better, you're grounded. Stay here, haunt your rooms, watch the world pass you by...and become Louisa all over again. Your choice, of course."

There was a knock at the door. When Timothy opened it, Cole handed him Janiss's coat and a bag of other items she assumed came from her car.

"Is she all right?" Cole asked, looking across the room at her.

"Yes," Timothy answered, waving him off. "Your chivalry is duly noted." He set the bag of items inside the door and turned to Janiss with the coat. "Did you want this right now?"

She considered it, then shook her head. Timothy set her coat down with the bag and went back to his papers.

Janiss felt she had every right to be depressed – and none of it was anything she was going to get over quickly. She was twenty-two years old and would stay that age, maybe forever; but what was she going to do with herself?

"I guess being a school teacher is out," she lamented. "Teaching elementary school at night would be difficult with all the students at home asleep."

Eating the students wouldn't help, either.

Timothy finished milling about and sat down next to her. "Was there anything else you wanted to do with your life before your death?"

That was at least twice he had tried to be funny. "Stop that. It's not like you." She thought about his question. "I used to pretend I was an archeologist when I was little. I'd find a rock down by the creek and imagine it was a fossil or an arrowhead or something."

"Indiana Jones or Lara Croft?"

"I know. It's stupid."

Timothy grinned. And not one his patronizing grins, either. "There's a reason our motif was chosen for the landing seal and lobby designs. Besides the medical research and work with the elderly, we were also starting to look into the origins of vampires."

Research sounded interesting and she was good at that. "The Mayan stuff? What for?"

"Aztec. We were looking for ways she could destroy Ian or any vampires she might run across, if necessary. We learned about a blood cult, entire nations that practiced bloodletting and ritualistically sacrificed children."

Janiss frowned. "All this talk is going somewhere positive, I hope?"

"As a matter of fact, yes. Would you like the tour?"

Chapter 54

In the dark hallway at the bottom of the central elevator, the silver-metallic door into the training room was sealed shut again. Timothy indicated the last normal door at the end of the hall, just to the left of it and stepped aside.

Janiss turned the knob and peered in.

The first thing she noticed was an ornate mirror set into an ironwork frame. It was mounted on a wall made from a smooth gray-and-white flecked stone, polished to a reflective shine. A table beneath the mirror and a couple of benches were made of the same material, as was the floor and ceiling.

The architecture combined the elements of an office building and a spacious mausoleum, perfect for the up-and-coming vampire business professional. The hallway continued on into a larger space. Following a blue-gray carpeted walkway into the interior, Janiss got her first real look at what Louisa had called home.

"This is the atrium," Timothy said, following her in.

It was breathtaking.

The enormous space was an oval-shaped chamber; the carpeted walkway ringed the outer edge of it. In the center was a sunken living room beneath a domed ceiling. Along the outer wall, around the walkway, were at least a dozen doors made of stained glass set into iron frames; each design was a little different than the rest. A double entry, also stained glass, was centered at the back of the atrium behind two black long tables with high-backed chairs. The floors, walls and ceilings were all made of the same flecked stone material. Electric lights made to look like pillar candles were set into iron sconces between the entryways and in the back corners.

Two silver-metallic doors – she guessed those were the other two entries into the training room – were clearly visible in the front of the atrium. Set onto the wall between them was an enormous television screen; the seating throughout the room was angled for optimal viewing. There was a compact kitchen in the opposite corner from the vestibule.

Timothy stepped down into the living room by one of the three short stairways. Plush white couches were situated in a semicircle surrounded a black, glass-top coffee table. As he touched the tabletop, a keyboard illuminated through the glass; the entire surface acted like a touch screen. The giant television screen came to life, showing a grid of security camera feeds from all over the facility.

Janiss grinned. "Really?"

Timothy shrugged. "She loved her gadgets. We have to keep a tech on site most of the time to ensure all of them stay updated and working."

"Sounds a little obsessive."

He touched another illuminated symbol on the glass and all of the screens went dark again. "There's a secure pass-through from the kitchen into guest room eight. Bathrooms are on either side of the atrium, one next to the kitchen and the other next to the coatroom in the vestibule. There's also a study, small library, media room, storage rooms and two smaller guest rooms."

For who? He'd also failed to mention the double doors at the back.

"Where did she sleep?" Janiss asked.

The moment she said it, it felt weird. Both she and Timothy had been avoiding calling Louisa by name, but it wasn't as if she could stop thinking about her. It had only been a few hours earlier that Louisa had said goodbye and Janiss felt more like an intruder than her successor.

Stepping in between the long tables at the back, Timothy unlatched the double doors. They opened into a round bedchamber equal in size to the training room, but with the walls and ceiling similar to the atrium. There was a pinwheel pattern etched into the middle of the floor instead of the carpeting that was everywhere else. Centered in the back across from the double doors was an antique four-poster bed, complete with pillows, linens, and drapes. Matching dressers, end tables, and trunks completed the room.

Pulling the master bedroom doors closed, Timothy indicated the two other rooms. "A full bath is on the left and a walk-in closet is on the right."

Was that all? It couldn't be.

It wasn't enough to be underground; a vampire had to be *in* the ground when at rest.

When Janiss looked back at Timothy to ask about that, she caught him staring intently at a section of the wall. A leafless tree with flowery blossoms was etched into it.

There were four such carvings in the room, each identical to the others and positioned right across from one another. At a glance, they seemed to be mere decoration.

Looking satisfied that he had her attention, Timothy stepped over to the first carving. He pressed one of the blossoms, then did the same to the second, third, and fourth, a different flower on each. A sound came from beneath the bedchamber just before the pinwheel pattern in the floor began to sink into a spiral staircase.

Janiss sighed and shook her head.

"Don't judge," Timothy scolded as he led the way down.

The bottom of the spiral staircase emptied into a dark passageway. Sconces holding flaming torches illuminated the path. The use of actual fire seemed a bit theatrical, especially if they were lit all the time.

"Natural gas?" Janiss asked.

Timothy nodded. "West Virginia's finest."

The passage opened into a crypt dominated by the surprising sight of a sarcophagus.

It was a solid piece of white stone, almost two feet thick and topped with the carving of a nondescript woman in a full dress clutching a long sword.

The sarcophagus was surrounded by eight round columns that cast ominous shadows in the flickering torchlight. The ceiling of the crypt mirrored the structure of the sunken living room above it. While the effect was unnerving to her, it bothered her more that the truly monstrous thing in the crypt was actually her.

"What do you think?"

Janiss glanced around the room and shrugged. "I think all it's missing is a magic mirror and a bowl of poisoned apples." She looked down at the sarcophagus. "How does this open? I don't see a lid or cover."

"Stay here."

Timothy walked back over to where the passage entered the crypt and faced the sarcophagus. He glanced down at the brick floor, then walked back toward Janiss while stepping intentionally onto four specific stones. There was a loud click from the sarcophagus.

"Push it open."

As Janiss pushed on the edge of the stone, it moved across easily over a section of the floor, revealing a shallow grave down into a bed of earth. The look of it reminded her of the cellar, a place she inexplicably didn't fear in spite of everything that had happened to her there.

"On the inside of the capstone is a steel bar," Timothy explained. "Once you're closed up inside, turn the bar clockwise to lock it. All of this is yours now."

She glanced around. Louisa had left her a fully functional subterranean vampire lair, complete with secret crypt. It wasn't the worst place to spend all of eternity, just as long as she was allowed out once in a while.

As she glanced back, Janiss caught a melancholy look from Timothy. He was staring into the empty grave as though remembering. Pushing his papers and staying busy might have kept his thoughts from Louisa, but she could tell he was affected by her absence.

"So," Janiss began, intending to distract him, "how does the Foundation make enough money to support all of this?"

Timothy blinked a few times before answering. "It doesn't." He immediately took out his phone, tapped it a few times, and showed her a list of items with numbers beside them. "There's no such thing as a poor old vampire. Her holdings and investments were substantial."

Janiss was impressed, both with the numbers and the way he recovered. "Now they're mine?"

Timothy's sarcastic grin made a reappearance, too. "The estate belongs to the Foundation along with all assets."

"Including me, I'm guessing."

"You will receive a weekly stipend while you're here," he continued, ignoring the comment. "If you choose to leave, a severance has been allotted based on your time of stay."

"Choices are good..."

He showed her the screen again.

"...and that's a lot of decimal places," she whispered, as though it were a closely guarded secret. "I don't suppose we own a private jet?"

"No," Timothy said with a droll tone. "We own one-sixth of a private jet."

"So, I could do whatever I want as long as I fulfill my obligations here?"

"Essentially. I'll explain the requirements and arrange your schedules. Concessions can be made as you see fit upon request, provided there's time or unless some other conflict arises. I'm awfully good at scheduling."

"What about this archeology thing you mentioned

upstairs?"

Timothy led Janiss back out of the crypt and up into the media room. Several large screens were mounted on the wall along with smaller ones at a lower level. At the touch of a key, the screens illuminated and prompted for a password. Timothy entered it and opened a file marked with another goggle-eyed fang face.

A picture appeared on the monitors, a still image of what Janiss presumed to be a warrior. It was drawn on a piece of yellowed parchment and looked very old. The figure wore a green-feathered headdress and had a goggle-eyed face or mask with fangs. A shield was carried in one hand and something that resembled a crooked stake was in the other.

"Meet Tlaloc. He was a god of water and earth, sometimes depicted living underground or in caves. In return for blood sacrifices, often children, he made the rains come. Sound familiar?"

Janiss couldn't help but think that both Daniel and her father would have been intrigued by all of this. "I thought vampires were a Christian myth."

"A modern interpretation, perhaps. Since we both know vampires aren't a myth, perhaps Tlaloc wasn't a myth, either."

"I'm not a fan of the child sacrifice thing. Did Louisa ever mention anything about that?"

When Janiss accidentally said Louisa's name, Timothy didn't react. "As in a special liking for the blood of children? She said she didn't like children and actively avoided them."

It made sense. "Or she liked them very much and needed to avoid them."

"There's more," Timothy added, "myths the world over. Louisa was compiling data for a research center. We've already started compiling artifacts in a nearby warehouse. We were just about to break ground on the south end of the facility behind the Sanctum. We were calling it Phase Three."

Now *he* had said her name once and it didn't feel as weird. "Catchy. Are we trying to kill vampires off?"

Timothy shook his head. "Trying to understand what they are and how they fit in the world. They're not demons or of the Devil. The Tlaloc legends suggest that they may have been tribal priests or guardians. Perhaps that was their reason for being."

"When they weren't eating children."

"Of course."

Janiss needed time. There was so much she needed to put behind her, to get over and get past, but this could be her future. In spite of everything, the idea did interest her, even if she didn't always travel to exotic locations and crack a bullwhip while holding onto her hat.

She was also concerned about being alone, something that neither Louisa nor Ian had ever got past.

It hurt thinking about Daniel and what might have been, and knowing his parents had a body to bury didn't exactly instill her with a sense of closure.

"So, how does one book a flight on one-sixth of a private jet?"

Chapter 55

Almost a week had passed.

On Thursday evening just before seven, a twin-engine Gulfstream jet touched down at Alderman Airport just outside of St. Clairsville, Ohio. Thirty minutes later, a black limousine arrived at Union Cemetery on the northeast side of the city. Lights had been put up on the grounds for the nighttime funeral, along with a tent, and mourners were already gathering by the time the limo arrived.

Inside the car, Janiss found the intercom button for the driver and pushed it. "Let's wait for a moment, please."

"Yes, ma'am," a voice answered.

"I still don't know why we needed Travis and Cole," Janiss complained to Timothy.

"Security," he replied. "You're an asset now, remember? Assets require protection. You're the administrator of Cedarcrest Sanctum and the figurehead for the Foundation. Security is a privilege, not a curse."

"Who are they going to protect me from? I could probably kick both their asses if I put my mind to it, even after they ghoul up."

"Ouch." It sounded like Travis over the intercom. Cole was stifling a laugh.

Janiss looked down. The switch was a push-on and

push-off type, not a momentary-on switch. The tiny red intercom light was still on.

"Damn it," she said under her breath and pushed the button again, watching for the light to go off. "I guess I shouldn't be too surprised later when ninja assassins slip past them and kill me."

Timothy grinned but said nothing.

"I'm still not sure about this," she whispered.

"You're fine. If things get tough, signal any of us. Your phone will ring and you can excuse yourself back to the car. If you think you can't recover afterward, we'll leave."

"Sounds like meeting a blind date."

Timothy didn't remark and waited patiently.

Janiss continued. "Last week when I called my dad, he said he was happy I was trying to start a meaningful relationship so that I didn't wind up like Sis Linn."

"But?"

Janiss gestured at her clothes. "Here I am, wearing a black power suit, the supposed administrator of her clandestine little facility, a blood-sucking creature of the night, and going to see my parents in a cemetery. How have I not become Louisa?"

Timothy turned toward her. "First of all, your parents are still alive. Second, toward the end, there was nothing Louisa feared more than leaving Cedarcrest. She didn't want to be a part of the world anymore."

Ian did, Janiss thought, but he also like setting fire to things.

"You're not alone, Janiss. This is brave of you.

Louisa would have never attempted anything like this."

"Maybe that makes me an idiot. I'm still afraid I'm going to kill someone. Maybe everyone."

"Risk brings reward. You can do this."

There it was, the combined philosophies of her vampire stepparents.

Janiss nodded, took a deep breath, and opened the door.

Everyone else got out with her and headed toward the small crowd gathered at the funeral. For a moment, Janiss imagined Felicia narrating one of her animal programs on television.

"The prey animals seemed to sense the lioness had recently fed, unsuspecting she would still happily devour three or four more of the slower members of the herd."

Travis and Cole stood on the edges of the crowd and did their job, watching for anything suspicious, while Janiss and Timothy mingled. Everyone there was in black. One person stood out, a man dressed in a US Navy crackerjack uniform.

Asking Timothy to hang back, Janiss approached Daniel's older brother. "Eric?" She had forgotten he was taller than his younger sibling.

The clean-shaven young man turned around. "Janiss Annette Connelly." His tone seemed pleasant enough. "It's been years."

She smiled back as best she could. "You look good. How's the Navy? Still making it a career?"

"Same as ever; I'm coming up on eight years. If I re-up, I might as well do my twenty." He noticed what

Janiss was wearing over her suit and raised an eyebrow. "Is that my old pea coat?"

"Daniel left it at my Gramma's house the last time I saw him." Janiss meant to say more or ask if he would mind if she kept it, but she had to stop herself. It would have been difficult to explain why her eyes were bleeding. At least the coat was a distraction from looking at Eric's exposed neck where it met his shoulder.

"Do you know what happened to him?" He looked cautiously curious.

Janiss bit her lip, then took a breath. "I invited him to go with me out to the nursing home, the Tuesday night before Thanksgiving."

It was the same lie she had told her mother over the phone. Her father had been strangely unavailable for that call, but she didn't mind since she expected to come clean with him after the funeral. Lying to her mom was tough, but lying to her father was impossible. Eric was somewhere in between.

"He didn't go with you?"

Janiss shrugged. "You know how he hates those places and it was late by the time I got back. I thought he was already asleep in the back bedroom – and then I ended up falling asleep on the couch. He wasn't there the next morning, so I thought he might have gone to town for something."

Eric looked like he was thinking about it, maybe a little too hard. "Did you have a fight?"

"No." The question blindsided Janiss. "Why would you ask that?"

"It doesn't sound like him. Unless there was some other reason, he still would have ridden in the car with you – even if he had to wait."

Janiss hoped the guilt that must have been on her face looked more like sorrow. "I wish he would have. I didn't find a note and there was no answer on his phone. I'm so sorry, Eric. It's insane what happened."

Eric bristled with anger but didn't say anything else. She wasn't exactly sure what upset him but supposed it didn't matter.

Against her better judgment, Janiss risked putting her arms around him and pulling him close. It felt good to hold him, someone she knew and trusted. She didn't realize how much it would comfort her until she felt his arms close around her in return. He seemed to need it as much as she did; but the longer she held him, the more it felt like betrayal.

"I would give anything to trade places with him," she whispered into his ear. "I mean that."

Without another word, Eric nodded and gently pushed her away before walking off alone into the cemetery.

Timothy stepped closer to Janiss as she watched him go. "See? No worries."

"I've got enough for the two of us," she corrected.

"Janiss!" she heard the familiar voice of her mom call out. Her mother and father were walking toward the both of them. Her father looked stern.

Janiss leaned closer to Timothy. "This is my mom and dad. Try to act human."

"You, too," he replied, stepping forward to intercept them. "Mr. and Mrs. Connelly? I'm Timothy Harker with the Cedarcrest Foundation." He put his hand out for her father to shake.

"Harker?" Mr. Connelly's face relaxed as he graciously accepted the handshake. "You don't arrange estate purchases for vampires, do you?"

"Only in and around London, sir," Timothy replied.

Janiss shuddered, but Timothy grinned knowingly.

Even having no idea what there were joking about, Janiss could tell her father had switched into "first impression" mode, his opening sales tactic. A moment after, she caught the look she was afraid of: the serious glance she always got when she knew she was in trouble. At least he was being cordial for the time being; but she suspected their talk after the funeral wasn't going to go pleasantly.

Distracted by her father, her mom almost tackled her into an embrace before trying in earnest to crush her. "I was horrified when I heard. We never should have let the two of you go out there."

It looked like her mom was going to cry – and that, in turn, would have made Janiss cry. Ever at the ready, Timothy handed Janiss a black handkerchief, something that wouldn't reveal anything red with which it might come into contact. Janiss genuinely appreciated the forethought as she accepted it.

"The media is eating it up," her mother continued. "They're calling him the 'Congregation Killer,' or something. Don't they realize they're glorifying him?" She looked at her daughter, then appeared concerned. "I thought you'd look sadder, Sweetie. You looked – haunted."

"I've been crying for a week, mom." That was true. "I don't think I have any tears left." That was also true.

"I'm still concerned about you not graduating next year," Mr. Connelly said. "Your student teaching was all you had left to finish. That's kind of why we got you the new car."

Her poor little sacrificial car.

Timothy stepped in for the save. "We made Ms. Connelly a very generous offer; but the timeframe was very limited for our replacement. We're grateful that your daughter came highly recommended and was willing to come on board with us on such short notice. The Foundation encourages all employees to continue their education while in our employ."

Wow, Janiss thought. He was a pretty good schmoozer; but she could tell her father didn't like what he was hearing.

Then the big problem appeared. Daniel's parents spotted Janiss and her folks talking with Timothy. Sean, Daniel's dad, looked stable; but his mother, Marie, looked on edge. Janiss clenched the handkerchief Timothy had given her and prepared for the worst.

"Hello, Mr. Moore," Janiss said to Daniel's dad. "I'm so sorry this happened."

Sean leaned in to give Janiss a quick hug, but Daniel's mother cut him off. She stood right up to Janiss, a little shorter and having to look up, livid with anger. "This wouldn't have happened if he hadn't been there with *you*."

Janiss looked devastated and tried to hold in the tears. Marie was right, of course. Still, Janiss's mother came to her daughter's rescue.

"My daughter is every bit as devastated by this as you are, Marie." Her tone was sincere but protective.

Marie scowled at them both.

Janiss tried to apologize again. "I'm sorry, Mrs. Moore..."

She pointed her finger at Janiss and shook it. "You're still wearing his coat!"

Mr. Moore took his wife by the shoulders. "We all lost someone here today."

In spite of her best efforts, Janiss turned away to dab her eyes. She saw Timothy reach for his phone, but she caught his eye and lightly shook her head before he dialed.

"Please keep the coat, Janiss," Mr. Moore continued, "and thank you and your family for helping cover the costs for the funeral and a headstone."

Janiss nodded. "Thank you for delaying the service so I could be here."

At that instant, a car peeled out and away from the funeral. It looked like an old Mustang. Eric used to own one of those.

Marie looked back at Janiss. "Now Eric's run off. What do you have to say about that?"

"There's nothing I can say to bring Daniel back,"

Janiss said in as sincere a tone as she could.

Marie froze. Hearing her dead son's name had an impact. She stepped forward, put her hand on Janiss's shoulder as if she was about to say something, then shook her head and walked away.

The rest of the service was civil. It looked like it might rain, but it didn't. Janiss declined to speak. It would have been impossible for her.

When it was over, the small crowd dispersed until only a few remained: Janiss, her parents and Timothy among them. Janiss had agreed to go over to her parents' house for a while, maybe collect a few personal belongings and talk. She couldn't stay the night.

There was one thing left to do before leaving the funeral; it was the reason she had come at all. Janiss left the others behind and walked over to stand close to Daniel's closed coffin.

"I'm sorry," she whispered. "I was just starting to imagine what spending the rest of my life with you might have been like. Then someone took that away and turned me into this. I killed you,and I can never take it back."

A bolt of lighting silently arced through the shadowy clouds across the sky. A light rain started to fall.

She felt a presence. She didn't have to look to imagine it was Daniel standing just behind her, even if she knew it was only in her mind. It was his voice she heard in her head.

"The last thing I thought before I died...I was happy you were safe."

He put his hand on her shoulder.

She turned and looked. Daniel wasn't there.

Of course, he wasn't. He was in the coffin in front of her.

"I'm going to find as many of them as I can," Janiss said. "The makers and their progeny. I don't know how yet, but I'm going to do whatever I have to keep them from turning into what destroyed us.

"Goodbye, Daniel. Wish me luck."

www.ingramcontent.com/pod-product-compliance
Lightning Source LLC
Chambersburg PA
CBHW072205170626
46813CB00003B/794